FILTHY LAWYER

FORBIDDEN SERIES

BIANCA COLE

Book Cover Design by Deliciously Dark Designs

❀ Created with Vellum

CONTENTS

1. Ivy — 1
2. Ivy — 9
3. Wes — 19
4. Ivy — 27
5. Wes — 37
6. Ivy — 43
7. Wes — 55
8. Ivy — 63
9. Wes — 71
10. Ivy — 77
11. Wes — 85
12. Ivy — 95
13. Wes — 111
14. Ivy — 121
15. Wes — 127
16. Ivy — 137
17. Wes — 153
18. Ivy — 165
19. Wes — 173
20. Ivy — 189
21. Wes — 197
Epilogue — 209

Also by Bianca Cole — 219
About the Author — 223

IVY

*T*he pitter-patter of rain hitting the floor to ceiling glass window echoes around my father's office. I watch the water cascade down the glass. It's not late, but the dark clouds outside make it feel like dusk.

I sigh, dreading the firm's quarterly party tonight. Once every three months, my dad arranges a party for partners and clients. I'm not even a partner at the firm, but my dad insists I attend.

A shudder passes through me, thinking about the last party a few months ago. Adrian, a client of the firm, groped my ass. He is seventy-seven years old. Twenty-seven years older than my father and more than triple my twenty-three years.

It was gross. All the men at these work parties are

perverts. They think because I'm a woman, they can grope me, no matter who my father is.

The thought of attending another party makes my stomach twist.

"Ivy," my dad booms, snapping me from my train of thought. "Are you even listening to me?"

My eyes meet my father's dark gaze. "Of course."

His eyes narrow. "What did I say?"

I bite my lip, and my shoulders slump. "I'm sorry. I'm distracted because I *really* don't want to attend the party tonight."

My dad's jaw clenches. "Ivy, how many times do we have to have this discussion?"

I swallow hard. "I know. I'm the future managing partner of this company and have to make an appearance."

His rage eases. "Exactly." He lets out a long sigh. "I know it isn't easy for you, a woman working in a male-dominated environment. The thing is, sweetheart, you've got to own it and toughen up."

I give him a weak nod, averting his gaze. I know my father wishes he had a boy. It would make his life much easier. My parents weren't sure whether they could have children at all. They were successful, and my mom gave birth to me, but they couldn't have any more children. It meant my dad had to accept I was all he was getting.

It didn't stop him from forcing me into law and priming me to take over his position at the law firm. I never wanted to be a lawyer. I *despise* it. The thing is, what I wanted never mattered. From a young age, there was no question. I was studying law, and that was the end of it.

When I was seventeen, I had a rebellious streak and told my father I was going to be an author instead. That was short-lived, though. He threatened to disown me. I caved and went to law school.

He would never understand what it was like for me working at the firm. How could he? He is always so wrapped up in his work. He never notices what happens around him. Every single one of his partners and male clients sees me as a piece of meat. The last party wasn't an isolated incident. It's rare I can get through one without being groped or objectified.

His drive and obsession with the firm only got worse when my mom left. She left him for another man two years ago. I rarely see her anymore. She's off somewhere in Europe, living her life and forgetting about the both of us.

"I don't want to hear any more whining." He tightens his tie around his neck. "Now, get back to work for the afternoon, and I will see you tonight." He glares at me.

I push up from the chair and turn, leaving his office without another word. It doesn't even make sense for me to go to these parties. I'm a junior lawyer, not a partner. He makes it worse, not letting me bring Scarlet, my best friend, along anymore. Apparently, she's not refined enough for his stupid parties.

A smile plays at my lips as I recall the first and last time she attended one with me. We both got drunk, but she was totally and utterly ruined. By the end of the night, she was up on the table, dirty dancing. Scarlet has always been a lightweight, and the men were quick to offer her glass after glass of champagne.

Sure, it was a *bad* move dancing on the tables, but I didn't hear any of the partners or clients complaining in the slightest—most of them were egging her on. That's what they want, young girls dancing on tables, who they can objectify and grope. I'd never understood why my dad banned her from the parties *ever* since.

I let out a long sigh, flopping into my desk chair, and leaning back. The sea of files on my desk makes me cringe. I've got too much work to do, and I hate every damn minute of it.

My grandfather founded this law firm, and my father is desperate to keep it under family control.

Hence, I'm stuck doing something I loathe day in and day out. And don't get me started about the hours, because they're ridiculous. I can't even remember the last time I had a holiday.

Sam, my secretary, pops her head through the door. "Hey, Ivy, do you have a minute?"

I nod. "Of course. What's up?"

She steps into my office, clutching a piece of paper in her hand. "Your father's secretary asked me to pass along your invite for the party tonight." She hands me the paper.

I glance down at the invite and huff, wishing I could be anywhere but at that party tonight.

Sam clears her throat, bringing my attention back to her. "Is everything all right?" Her dark brown eyes search my face. I can't keep anything from Sam.

"Yeah… It's just I hate these events. I wish he didn't make me attend."

Her brow raises. "What's so bad about them?"

"I'm not a fan of being groped and gawked at by men as old or older than my father."

Her brow raises. "It doesn't sound all bad. I wouldn't mind being groped by rich men."

I laugh. "I wish you could take my place, then."

"I would in a heartbeat. I've not been getting much

action. It's difficult for a single woman in her forties, you know."

"You don't understand how gross it is." I shake my head. "At the last party, a seventy-seven-year-old groped my ass. He was old enough to be my grandad, and it made me feel sick."

She crinkles her nose. "Okay, that sounds gross. I thought you meant guys in their fifties."

"Well, even that is too old for me." I shrug. "I don't want to be touched by a man the same age as my dad." I let out a long sigh and rest my head on my arms, folding them on the desk. "It is the same every time. My dad insists it is important for me to attend because he's priming me to become a managing partner, which is ridiculous."

"Why is it ridiculous?"

I glance up at her. "This industry isn't built for women to be in power. Not to mention, the Heisman firm is one of the most male-dominated workplaces ever." I let out a long, shaky breath. "I never even wanted to be a damn intellectual property lawyer," I grumble.

She sighs. "Then why don't you tell your father that? Surely, he would listen to you."

"I've told him countless times, but he doesn't take me seriously," I say.

Sam perches on my desk like she often does. "It's about time that man did take you seriously. You're a strong, independent woman."

I smile. "Thanks, Sam, but that will never happen. I'm a lawyer, and nothing will ever change."

She tilts her head to the side. "If you think like that, then sure, nothing will ever change." She shakes her head. "Ivy, it's your life. You have the opportunity to seize control. No one can control you. You should never believe there isn't a way out."

"I know." I run my hair through my fingertips, glancing at it. "I've spent so much money to become a lawyer. I'm up to the hilt in debt. I couldn't even afford *not* to be one." I wince at that.

Sam sighs. "I still can't believe your father didn't pay for your tuition."

"He wants to teach me responsibility."

She clicks her tongue. "Bullshit. He wants to make sure you've got no choice but to be a lawyer because of money."

My eyes widen at her bluntness. Sam has been my secretary since I started here, two years ago, and we became good friends. "Maybe." I bite my lip, wondering if my dad really is that calculating. "Do you think he would do that?" I blink a few times.

Sam lets out a long breath. "I don't know, Ivy." She

squeezes my hand. "All I know is your father is a highly driven individual, and I wouldn't put it past him."

A weight settles on my chest at the thought. My father has always been driven, but if she is right about his motivations not to pay my tuition, then that makes him cold-hearted. Deep down, he knows I don't want to be a lawyer. He knows I wouldn't have chosen this life for myself.

I don't know if he would have been so calculating as to trap me in this life, though.

2

IVY

hat can I get you, sweetheart?" The barman winks at me.

Great.

Even the barman at this party is sleazy. "Gin and tonic, please."

He flashes me a smile before walking off and getting my drink. What is wrong with the men in this place? At least he isn't old. That's something, I guess. I look to the left and notice an older man staring at me. He has to be about seventy, staring at my ass. My stomach twists with sickness as he smiles at me, raising his eyebrow.

My lunch threatens to make a terrible reappearance as my stomach churns. I hate these events more and more with each one.

The barman returns. "Here you go, beautiful." He passes me the gin and tonic, sliding a napkin across the bar with his number scribbled over it.

"Thanks, but…" I push the napkin back toward him. "I'm not interested."

His mouth tightens into a straight line as I move away to a quieter spot by the bar. As soon as my father sees me, I plan to head home early. He can't keep tabs on me *all* night. It's a solid plan.

Why does my stomach twist with dread?

I know why. These parties never go that smoothly. I sip my drink as I scan the room, searching for my dad. Instead, I spot the asshole who groped me last time, making my skin crawl.

Where is he?

The sooner I see him and speak to him, the sooner I go home. I keep scanning the room for him, searching the sea of gray hair. My attention stops on a man with blonde hair staring right at me. A charming smile tugs at his lips as he watches me from over the other side of the room.

For the first time, there's a handsome guy here at one of my father's shitty parties. I let my eyes rake down his body. He's well dressed in a black form-hugging suit. He's not much older than me, perhaps in his late twenties.

I avert his gaze and turn back to the bar, sipping on my drink. I tighten my grip on the glass in my hand and turn back to face him. He's still staring at me as the guy next to him keeps chatting.

It's been a long time since I've been with a man. Ever since my ex-boyfriend, Alec, dumped me, I've kept my distance from men.

It's about time I push it into my past and focus on having some fun. Perhaps, if I have a chat with this guy and see where it goes, it will stop any other creeps groping me tonight. I take another long sip of my drink, draining the last drop. I scan my eyes across the room, searching for my dad one more time. I still can't see him.

What the hell, I might as well let my hair down.

I set my glass down on the bar and then turn back to face the handsome guy on the other side of the room. I walk away from the bar toward him, taking a few steps with my eyes fixed on him. My heart skips a beat as he says something to the man he'd been talking to and walks toward me too, smiling.

I'm half-way across the room when a pair of hands grab my hips, pulling me to a stop and into a hard, muscled body.

What the hell?

A strong scent of bourbon and cologne fills my

nostrils. Whoever has me snakes his arm around my waist, pulling me back hard against him. I shift, glancing at the man holding me.

He's ridiculously handsome with a strong, wide jaw and dark brown stubble peppering it. His eyes focus on the man in front of him, but I can see they are dark brown.

His large hand settles on my stomach, lingering there as if owns me. I *gasp*, shocked at the way this guy is holding me.

Who the hell does he think he is?

My eyes flick back to the man I'd been approaching. He's on the other side of the room with the man he'd been speaking with. He is glaring over here, looking pissed.

Great.

The man holding me against him speaks, but not to me, "Sorry, what were we talking about?"

The man in front of us glances between this guy and me, eyes wide.

I push against this asshole's hard chest, trying to break free from him. "What the *fuck* do you think you are doing?"

He is so strong I can't get out of his grip. As if I haven't even spoken, he continues chatting to the guy in front of us, blanking me.

My heart rate spikes as his hand slides to cup my ass through my dress. That does it. I push him harder this time, breaking free from his grip. "Get the fuck off *me*."

The asshole who groped me turns and frowns. "What the hell is wrong? Aren't you all paid up for the night, *sweetheart?*"

What the fuck?

The men standing around us all go silent and watch on in horror. Most of them would recognize me. Most people in Wynton would recognize me because of my father. Who the hell is this guy to mistake me for a fucking prostitute?

"Are you kidding me?"

He narrows his eyes. "Don't speak to me like that." He reaches for me again and pulls me into him, lowering his voice to a husky growl. "Or I'll make sure you never work in this town again."

I laugh and push him off me. "I hope this is all some joke."

He shakes his head, reaching to grab me for the *third* time. One time too fucking many on my count —enough is enough. Adrenaline pulses through my veins as I bring my hand up and slice it through the air, aiming for his face. I strike him, making a red mark prickle across his cheek. The slap of skin against skin echoes through the room. I wince as his prickly stubble stings my hand and my arm aches from the force of hitting him.

A deafening silence fills the room.

Shit.

I scan our surroundings to find everyone's eyes are on us. Thank God my father isn't here yet. Time seems to slow down as the asshole who groped me grabs hold of my hips possessively, forcing me toward him. His hand circles my wrist, and he drags me out of the room.

Once we're away from prying eyes, I turn toward him. "What the fuck do you think you're doing?" I writhe, trying to break free from his strong grasp.

He doesn't stop moving, dragging me along a hallway and into an empty room. My stomach dips, and the blood drains from my face. I'm alone with this creep, and he's insane. My body tenses as I switch into survival mode. I yank my arm free, spinning to face him and bringing my hand up to slap him again. At least, that was the plan.

He catches my hand mid-air, working out my intention before my hand gets anywhere near his face. He holds me where I am, glaring at me.

My breath catches in my throat as I take in his appearance. He is one of the most attractive men I've ever seen. His eyes are a dark and deep brown, blazing with fire as they fix on me. A stark contrast to the normal men that grope me at these parties—but he's as big of an asshole as the rest of them—may be the worst of the lot.

"I suggest you apologize right away," he growls.

I yank my arm from him and step back, resting my hands on my hips. "Are you fucking joking?" I shake my head slowly. "I'm not the one who should be apologizing."

He steps closer to me. "Do you know who I *am?*"

My eyes narrow. "Do you know who the *fuck* I am?"

He smirks at me with a cocky grin. "Yeah, you're the piece of ass paid up for my entertainment." He steps even closer. "Your job is to please the men, and I hate to break it to you, sweetheart, but you're not doing a great job.

Hot fiery rage rises inside of me, bubbling under the surface. I can't believe this guy mistook me for a prostitute. I glance down at my dress, wondering if I put on something racy by accident. My dress is conservative and classy. This guy is such an asshole. "I'm Ivy Heisman." I step closer to him. "Jack Heisman's daughter and a junior lawyer at the firm."

His grin widens, and he takes a step back. His eyes

rake down my body, making the rage bubble even more fiercely inside of me. The nerve on this guy is unbelievable. "Are you going to apologize for mistaking me for a hooker?"

His eyes darken with a fierce hunger as he steps closer, *again*. "Perhaps you should reconsider what you wear to these parties in the future." I glance down at my dress. It's a fucking navy blue maxi dress with a modestly plunging neckline. I can't wrap my head around how this guy mistook me for a hooker.

I open my mouth but shut it again, unable to find the words.

He takes another step, so there are only a few inches between us, towering over me. "I'm Wes, by the way. The new partner at your daddy's law firm."

Holy shit. Of course. Wesley Peterson has moved to Wynton from New York. He has an infamous reputation for being a playboy and a womanizer. My father told me he was hiring him, and when I looked him up online, the scandalous news reports mentioning him were endless.

He sets his hands on either side of my waist, making me tense. "Don't pretend you weren't turned on by the way I touched you."

Is this guy for real?

I step backward, away from him. "It made me feel physically sick."

He shakes his head. "You're a terrible liar. I bet your panties are soaked right through, darling." He winks at me.

Well, I thought I'd met the worst of the lot, but damn, was I wrong. This man is so arrogant and a complete and utter jerk. It seems like all the rumors in the press are *true*. Cocky isn't even a strong enough word to describe him. He's ridiculously attractive, but he knows it.

I cross my arms over my chest, drawing his eyes to my cleavage unintentionally. "What if I tell my father what you did?" I threaten, despite knowing my dad wouldn't believe me, anyway.

That fierce hungry look ignites in his eyes, sending a shiver down my spine. "I know you won't do that, sweetheart."

My jaw clenches. "Don't call me, sweetheart."

His smile widens. "Because, if you told your daddy, then you wouldn't be able to see this face every day at work."

Unbelievable.

My whole body shakes with rage. A volcano beneath my skin is bubbling and ready to blow. The hungry look

Wes gives me heats my body for a different reason. I open my mouth to give him a piece of my mind, but I can't. The rage consuming me is too furious that I can't speak. I spin on my heels, storming away from him without a word.

I don't care that my dad hasn't seen me at the party. I don't care that he'll give me shit about it. There's no way in hell I'm spending another minute at a party with that asshole. Netflix and a massive pot of Ben & Jerry's ice cream are *calling* to me. I'm going home. This party was worse than I ever expected.

3

WES

I'm screwed. Ever since last night, *all* I can think about is the managing partner's daughter, and it's my first day at the firm.

It's been about *twelve* hours since Ivy Heisman slapped me. *Twelve* hours since she took my brain hostage. I'm not used to being so consumed by thoughts of one woman.

Usually, I don't have a habit of thinking about women. I fuck them and forget about them. Sure, it might make me an asshole, but it's easier that way. No connections and no emotions mean no chance of getting hurt.

One slap later, and I'm sitting here in my new office thinking about her, unable to stop.

She's the sexiest, fiercest little thing I've ever met.

There's one problem. She's the managing partner's daughter—my boss's daughter. I can't fuck her. I'm pretty sure that is the best path to getting fired.

It doesn't help that this city is small. After living here all of two weeks, I'm sure the gossip wagon is harder to evade than New York. Everyone knows everything that happens here, and it spreads like wildfire.

I mean, look what happened to my friend Logan. It all worked out, but it's still in the papers a couple of weeks later. It's all anyone can talk about — the professor who dated his student. I *groan*, realizing how fucked I am right now.

Not to mention, I'm sure she hates me now. I pretended to mistake her for a prostitute. I had to stop her from talking to the guy across the room. The way he was looking at her made me angry.

The moment she stepped into that ballroom, I knew I had to have her. A fierce possessiveness clouded my mind, making me crazy.

All I can do is hope her father doesn't find out about what I did.

She's too beautiful and classy to be a prostitute. I knew that the moment I set eyes on her. Her fiery red hair is as *hot* as her attitude. Those bright blue eyes make me want to lose control and luscious pink lips that would fit perfectly around my *huge*, throbbing cock.

My secretary pokes her head through the door. "Sir, Jack Heisman wishes to see you in his office."

Shit.

I clear my throat. "Thank you, Ellen. Did he say when?"

She nods. "Right away, sir."

Perfect.

I adjust myself in my pants, ensuring my hard cock isn't too noticeable. I don't want to attend a meeting with the managing partner sporting a raging hard-on. I try to focus on anything but the daughter of the man who has summoned me to his office, and it softens a little. I stand from my desk and adjust my jacket before heading for the elevator.

Jack Heisman's office is on the top floor. I step into the elevator, tapping my foot on the floor, waiting for it to arrive. I walk past the secretary's desk, but no one is there. I clear my throat outside his door and then knock twice.

"Come in," he calls.

I turn the doorknob, opening my mouth to speak. I freeze the moment I notice the woman sitting opposite him. My dick thickens in my pants at the sight of that fiery, wavy red hair. It's unmistakable. She's unmistakable. *Ivy*.

I thrust my hands in my pocket, hoping that the creases in my trousers hide the fact that my cock is *very* hard again and throbbing against the zipper of my pants.

"Wes, thank you for coming." Jack stands. "Please come and meet my daughter." He gestures for Ivy to stand, too.

She gets to her feet and glares right at me. Her bright blue eyes are furious.

It looks like she hasn't forgotten our meeting the evening before. I plaster on my usual smirk. "Miss Heisman, it's a pleasure to meet a powerful woman such as yourself."

Her nostrils flare. She looks so beautiful when she's angry. "I can't say the same. Men in power always seem to think they can *take* whatever the hell they want."

I smirk at her no-shit attitude. She's as fiery as last night, and it's something I admire about her.

"Ivy, that's no way to speak to our newest partner at the firm," Jack says.

She grits her teeth. "It's a pleasure to meet you." There is no honesty in her words.

"I see you've dressed far more conservatively today." My eyes roam her tight blouse and navy skirt.

It's standard office wear, and I shouldn't be finding it sexy, but I have a feeling anything Ivy Heisman wears looks sexy.

"Oh, have you two already met?" Jack asks.

Ivy is glaring right at me. Little does she know it's only making me *harder*. "Yes, briefly at your party yesterday evening," she says, averting my gaze.

Jack clears his throat as the tension in the room hits a new high. "Anyway, I wanted to introduce the two of you officially. You are going to be working together on the Delaney case."

Ivy's eyes widen, and she spins toward her father. "Is that necessary? I've been handling the case fine by myself."

Jack turns to her. "Of course, Ivy. You are a junior lawyer at the firm, and Wes is our newest partner. I want the best person to introduce him to the law firm and work with him. I think you'll learn a lot from each other."

Shit.

I want to learn from her, but in such a *bad* way. I'm fucked. Working with Ivy on a case isn't going to be possible. The image of fucking her against the wall until she screams my name flashes through my mind.

My cock throbs at the image, leaking precum into the fabric of my boxer briefs. I try to adjust the pleats, hoping to high hell Jack can't tell I'm sporting a hard-on. Especially considering his daughter is the reason.

Although my move is subtle, Ivy's eyes flick right to my crotch.

Damn.

Her face turns the *prettiest* shade of pink, and her eyes snap back to my face.

I grin at her and raise an eyebrow.

It only ignites more fury in her eyes. "Is there anything else you need from me, father?"

Jack's attention moves to his daughter. "No, that's all, thank you, Ivy." He turns back to me. "Wes, I'd like to have a chat with you, though, if you don't mind?"

I nod. "Of course, sir."

Ivy storms passed me, focusing on anything but me. I shift so that her arm brushes against mine as she passes. I want to reach out and *grab* her, and if it weren't for her father watching me, I would have. The way she looked at me told me she wants to slap me again, and I'd welcome it. I think that's what has got me *so* hooked on her — the way she didn't take my shit.

"Wes, have a seat." He glances at the seat in front of his desk.

I take it and shuffle under his gaze. In this position, I'm no longer hard, thank God.

"I've got a few company documents for you to read and sign. We have the sexual harassment dossier, your employment contract, and the rules we abide by here at the Heisman firm." He passes me three large files.

I may have already violated the sexual harassment rules before even starting here. Jack doesn't need to know that, especially as his daughter was the woman I broke those rules over. I take the files and nod.

"If you can go through them this morning for me and hand them over signed to your secretary, that would be *perfect*," Jack says.

"Of course, sir." I adjust my tie. "Is there anything else?"

Jack's eyes narrow. "I've heard a lot about you, Wes. You're a fantastic lawyer, but make sure that when you're here at work, you keep it in your pants."

His warning makes my stomach twist. He has no idea how ironic it is.

"We have a strict no dating policy between employees because it can cause tensions and issues we don't want."

My tie feels too tight as I loosen it. This is *very* bad.

I'm not even sure I can abide by his rules when it comes to Ivy, his daughter. I hoped I could get over my infatuation when I saw her again, but after our brief encounter a moment ago, I *want* her more. How the fuck am I supposed to stay away from her now?

"Of course, sir," I reply, despite the warring conflict going on in my head.

He doesn't need to know that the likelihood of me keeping it in my pants is about *zero*. It's already straining against my zipper, desperate to become acquainted with Ivy, his daughter. He doesn't need to know that I want his daughter *more* than this damn job.

4

IVY

esley Peterson is an asshole—a *very* hot and handsome asshole. He has weaseled his way under my skin, and I can barely think of anything else. I haven't spoken to him since Monday at my father's introduction, but all he has to do is look at me, and he *pisses* me off.

This morning we were waiting for the elevator, and he objectified me, raking his eyes over my body with that irritating smirk on his face. I wanted to slap him all over again. Luckily, Sam was waiting there too. Otherwise, I'm sure he would have spoken to me.

He's the most arrogant man I've *ever* met. Not to mention unearthly handsome. It's not really a surprise he's so cocky, men who look like that always are.

He's tall and works out. I felt how hard and

muscular his body was when he pulled me against him, and his tight-fitting tailored shirts hug them *perfectly*. I bite my lip, thinking about the way his dark brown eyes burned with a fierce and hungry possessiveness this morning. The way he looks at me is as if he wants to *devour* me.

My thighs clench at the thought, and my panties soak through.

Damn it.

There's something *very* wrong with me. Not only does he piss me off, but he turns me on *all* at the same time.

Why can't I stop thinking about him?

He gets me hot under the collar with rage and irritating lust. It's totally out of my control. I sigh heavily, glancing at the pile of work on my desk, which only pisses me off more. All I want to do right now is curl up into a ball and go to sleep.

I shake my head, trying to knock myself out of the funk I've fallen into. A man shouldn't be able to derail me like this. He's not even worth thinking about. My work is more important, and I'm not going to let him get in the way of it.

The Delaney case file is on top of the pile, and I reach out for it. This is the case I have to work on with Wes. I need to make sure I know it inside and out. I don't want him to make me look bad. If anything, I'll try my damned hardest to make *him* look bad.

As I plow into the file, my irritation over Wes eases. The image of his smug face fades from my mind, and I get lost in my work. My attention is consumed by the case and nothing else. The rage that had been burning inside me turns to a *simmer* in the background.

I'm not sure how long I've been working when a knock at the door breaks my attention. "Come in."

A young woman enters clutching a file in her arms. "I've been told to bring you a case file that needs a draft document written up."

My brow furrows. It sounds like something that should be taken to the paralegal team. I gesture for her to bring it to me. She sets the papers down on my desk. I take one glance at the file and know this *isn't* meant for me. As a junior lawyer, it isn't something I deal with. "I think you've got the wrong office. I'm a junior lawyer, and this is below my pay grade. Are you sure you weren't supposed to take it to the paralegals?"

The girl's eyes widen, and the blood drains from her face. "I-I was following orders to bring them straight to you, Miss Heisman."

My eyes narrow. "Whose orders?"

"Mr. Peterson's." She shuffles on the spot. "I'm

Ellen, his assistant, and he told me he needs these doing urgently."

I shake my head, and the burning rage comes back *fiercer* inside of me. He is literally asking me to go and slap him again. "Thank you, Ellen. I will discuss the matter with Mr. Peterson."

She bites her lip before nodding and walking out of my office. My entire face flushes hot. If he wants a fight, then a fight he is going to get. I stand up from my desk, trembling.

My fists clench around the file as I step out of my office and down the hallway toward Wes' office. Normally, I've got patience. Anger isn't an emotion I'm used to feeling, but this man knows how to push my buttons. Wes gets under my skin like no one *ever* has.

I step around the corner to his office, and Ellen locks eyes with me, swallowing hard. Without even knocking, I storm into his office. There's no way in hell I'm knocking for this asshole—he doesn't deserve the courtesy.

He glances up and smiles at me. "Ivy, to what do I owe this pleasure?" He leans back in his chair.

My lip trembles and my entire body shakes. I glare at him, taking a few steps forward toward his desk. Once I reach it, I throw the file down in front of him. "Why are you sending me work that is *way* below my pay grade? This is stuff the paralegal department deals with."

He laces his fingers behind his head. "I'm the partner on this case, and you're the junior lawyer. I can send you whatever work I *want*." That fierce hunger in his eyes burns as he sweeps his gaze down my body. It's as if this asshole is undressing me with his eyes. I can't understand why every time I'm near him, my panties soak through.

I grind my teeth together to stop from jumping across his desk and slapping him right here. "No," I *spit* out. "You can't assign me work." I cross my arms over my chest. "We're working together on this case. You're not my boss."

He leans forward, unlacing his hands from behind his head. "Ivy," he growls my name in a way that sends more heat right to my core. "I'm a higher rank than you, even if your daddy is the managing partner."

"You've just started here." I shake my head in disbelief. "It's not a secret that after what happened at the party, we're *never* going to get on." I point my finger at him. "How about you stay out of my way, and I'll stay out of yours?"

His eyes travel the entire length of my body, *again* spreading more fire through my veins. This guy is unbelievable. "No."

I shake my head. "What do you mean, no?"

His expression has turned serious. "I mean, *no*. We've been assigned to the same case. We're working together." He holds my glare.

"I can't work with *you*." I grind my teeth together. "You're the most infuriating man I've ever met."

He laughs and licks his lips. "Sweetheart, you're working with me whether you like it or not."

"One, my name is Ivy, not sweetheart. Two, we will see about that." I turn to leave. I need to get my father to take him off this case.

Wes gets up from his desk and comes after me. "Where are you going?" His hand circles my arm, jerking me to a stop.

I turn to face him. My body is shaking with pure rage and heat that his touch ignites inside of me. He's standing close to me, *too* close. His intense chocolate brown eyes search mine with that possessive look. My thighs tremble despite myself.

"I'm leaving," I mutter. Despite meaning it, I don't move.

He pins me to the spot with that stare. He takes another step forward, still gripping my arm. There's only an inch between us, and his warm breath falls on my face. My breath catches and heart *pounds* against my rib cage. My mouth has gone dry.

What the hell is wrong with me?

I should slap him again. I should push him away from me. Instead, I take a step backward. My back collides with the shut door.

He steps forward once more, trapping me against it. His hands slide onto my waist, and his warm, muscular body presses into me.

I can't move or speak. The way he is looking at me makes my pussy drip. I can feel it dampening my thighs. Wes is an asshole. He shouldn't be affecting me the way he is or getting me this wet.

He presses even closer, and his hard, throbbing cock grinds into my belly.

I *moan*, unable to stop myself. His smirk widens.

Damn.

I don't want to give this asshole the satisfaction. He does it again, making me feel every inch of his *huge* length pressing into me. I bite my lip to stop from moaning again.

The hunger in his eyes has taken over as he stares into mine. His lips aren't curled into an irritating smirk, and his expression is serious. I should want to slap him for pushing me up against a door, but all I want to do is *kiss* him.

It's impossible not to admire how handsome he is this close. He's the single most attractive man I've ever seen. The way he looks at me as if he can *take* whatever he wants makes me flushed with hot desire. And I want him to. I want him to *take* me right here.

No… It's so wrong.

I lick my bottom lip. "What the hell are you doing?"

His hands slip to my hips, pressing his fingers into me possessively. "Giving you what you want."

He grinds into me again with his *huge* length, and I almost cry out with need. I bite down hard on my lip, stopping myself.

"Get off me," I say weakly.

He moves closer and brushes his lips against my ear, sending a shiver down my spine. "Don't pretend you don't love being pressed up against me, Ivy." He moves one hand onto my bare thigh, moving higher. "Don't pretend you don't enjoy every inch of my thick, hard dick pressing into you." His large, rough hands brushing again my skin make me tremble. "Don't pretend that you're not soaking wet for me right now," he growls.

I capture my bottom lip with my teeth, but the *moan* still escapes me.

He *groans*, hooking a finger into my panties and sliding them to one side. His large finger *teases* between my slippery wet lips, parting them. "Naughty girl, you're so fucking wet," he growls.

I try pathetically to push him away.

"Don't pretend you aren't turned on. I can feel what I do to you." He slides his finger inside of me.

I bite down on my hand to stop from crying out. "That's it, baby. Let me finger that pretty little pussy." His other hand reaches around to cup my ass, and I whimper. He teases his thumb gently over my clit, and all reasoning leaves me. I *moan* deeply, arching my back and giving in to the sensation of his hands on me.

My eyes search his. That dark longing in his eyes makes me wetter still. His lips inch closer to mine, and we're crashing into each other. His finger still working at my clit as we bruise our lips together. His tongue flicks across my lips, and I part them eagerly. He teases my tongue with his own, searching my mouth. I *moan* into him. All my common sense is gone.

He grinds his thick, throbbing length against my lower tummy as we kiss. He has *ignited* a hot primal lust inside of me. All I want to do is fuck him right here, right now.

A *bang* outside his office door startles both of us. It snaps me right back to my senses. I *gasp*, pushing his body from me hard.

I glare at him for a few moments in utter shock. His

lips twist into that cocky smile that gets my blood pumping. "Don't you dare touch me ever again." I let myself out of his office and storm toward my own.

A mix of anger and pure sexual frustration floods me. He has got some nerve hitting on me like that. He also got me going like no man *ever* has. My panties are soaked through, dripping with my juices. My clit is aching and throbbing for release. I can't get over how *hot* that was. It shouldn't have been. Wes is that last man that should get me wet.

He has a reputation as a player and a womanizer. A reputation he just proved by forcing himself on me. If he wants to play *dirty*, then let's play. I intend to take him down a peg or *two*. If he thinks he can fuck anything that moves, he can think again.

It doesn't matter that my pussy is aching for his package, or throbbing from his touch. I can't stop thinking about how good it felt with his body pressed against my body and hands all over me.

It doesn't matter how good it would feel to have him bend me over his desk and *fuck* me hard.

No. I can't go there. This isn't about him.

It was just the situation that got me aroused, that, and the fact I haven't slept with anyone in over a year. Even if Wes was the last man on earth, I wouldn't fuck him.

5

WES

For the first time in my life, I'm desperate for a woman I *can't* have. My eyes are still glued to the spot Ivy had been standing in before she ran away from me. That file I sent to her office was bait. I knew it would piss her off, and she'd end up here.

She was turned on. I'd had her in my grasp, but she is one fiery woman with willpower like steel. Her tight little pussy was so fucking wet. I was ready to sink every inch of my aching cock deep inside of her. She was moaning as I kissed her. She wanted it as much as I did.

Why the fuck did she run off, leaving me leaning against the door with a raging hard-on?

I glance down at my tenting my suit pants before

turning the lock on the door. I cup my throbbing length through the fabric before unzipping the zipper and freeing myself from the restrictive confines of my boxers. My finger is still wet with Ivy's juices, and I slowly suck her sweet nectar from it, fisting myself with my other hand.

I *groan*, picturing Ivy's fierce blue eyes staring up at me. As I stroke my shaft in my hands, thick, white precum leaks from the tip, dripping onto the floor. Her tight, wet *pussy* felt better than anything I've ever felt wrapped around my finger. I long to feel it wrapped around my throbbing cock.

I wanted to push her down onto my desk, pull that little skirt up around her hips, and taste her pretty pussy. The way she moaned when I teased her clit was like music to my ears. I imagine my tongue teasing that throbbing, hard nub until she can't take it anymore. Until she comes all over my tongue, spilling her sweet juices *all over* my face.

My cock *twitches* in my hand as I tighten my grip and fist my length faster. Ivy Heisman has me wrapped around her little finger. She doesn't know it yet. I've never jerked off in my office before. I've *never* been so wound up over one woman. This primal urge to *claim* her and make her *mine* is so foreign to me.

Where the hell did it come from?

I *groan* loud, as the image of Ivy's plump lips parting and closing over the swollen head of my dick makes me harder. The thought of her taking my cock into her mouth and sucking on me makes my cum filled balls ache for release. I picture her totally naked, bobbing her head up and down my length.

In my fantasy, her perfect full breasts bounce, and her fiery eyes hold my gaze as she takes me all the way inside her throat.

I think of how good she would look bent over my desk, ass high and pussy nestled between her creamy thighs. The image makes my balls tingle. I bite my lip, trying not to make *too* much noise. I imagine how good it would be to take her like that—right here in my office. The thought of sliding every inch deep inside that tight, wet pussy makes me desperate for release.

I grunt as my balls clench. Thick, white cum pumps from the swollen crown, shooting rope after rope of it onto my office floor. The thought of pumping my seed deep inside Ivy makes me groan as I keep fisting. I keep running my hand from root to tip until every drop is out.

I glance down at the mess I've made.

Fuck.

My first week on the job, and I've unloaded my seed all over the office floor.

What is this girl doing to me?

I shove my softening dick back into my pants and grab some tissues, cleaning up my mess, before taking a seat behind my desk and shutting my eyes.

I've turned into some *primitive* man that can't stop thinking about taking and claiming this girl. It's not like I'm sexually frustrated or hard up for offers. Women often throw themselves at me. I never let feelings get in the way. When I'm with a woman, it's about sex and nothing else. It's easier that way.

But, with Ivy, it's different. I'm stroking my dick like a *horny* teenager over her in my office. I can't think of anything else since we met. It's like she has taken over my brain. The thought of any other man going anywhere *near* her makes me hot with rage.

Perhaps it was the way she slapped me when we first met. She took me down a notch. She won't take my shit, and it's refreshing. I knew she would be pissed when I sent that file down to her. It was an insult—an insult intended to bait her into my office. I was banking on her, storming in her, angry and glaring at me in a way that makes my cock throb in my pants.

I glance down to see my pants are tenting *again*. Ivy Heisman is going to be the death of me. No woman has ever run away from me like that.

At least now I know how much she wants me. She

tried to stifle her moans, but she couldn't. She kissed me like she was desperate for it.

My first week at the Heisman firm, and I should be thinking about how to secure my place here. Instead, it's Wednesday afternoon, and I'm formulating a plan to get the managing partner's daughter into my bed. There's no way I'm giving up on her this easily.

I'm not going to rest until I've claimed that fiery redhead's tight pussy. She's *mine*, and she better accept it before I go insane.

6

IVY

I couldn't think about anything but him. The way his large hands felt digging into my hips possessively. The way his lips claimed mine so fully. The way his huge cock felt pressed against my abdomen.

It's wrong how much I want him. I want to feel him against me *again*, even if he is an asshole—even if I hate him. My body *craves* his touch. The thrill of him pressing me up against his door was unlike anything I've ever felt.

I drive down the street toward my home on autopilot. Images of him kissing me and touching me flashing through my mind on repeat. To say I'm fucked is an understatement. Wes got under my skin the moment we met, but now he is under my skin for a different reason.

No man had *ever* kissed me the way he did. It was hard and passionate. A kiss I can't forget. I hate myself for wanting him the way I do. I know his reputation. He's a player—the last man in the world I should want. But my panties are still soaked through, and I'm so sexually frustrated it feels like I might combust.

It's only three in the afternoon, but I had to escape. I'm going insane over him, and I need to get home. My father was happy for me to work from home this afternoon. I need some space away from the office—away from him.

I pull into my building's parking lot and park up. I tuck the Delaney case file under my arm as I walk into my building. It's been impossible to get any work done since the incident.

I'm hoping a change of environment will clear my head and help me focus. This case is important. Perhaps, if I can make Wes look bad on the case, my father will reconsider his position at the firm. I need him out of my life before I do something I regret.

If he'd pushed me harder, I know I would have caved. I was so close to asking him to bend me over his desk and *take* me right there in his office. That can't happen. We *can't* happen.

I unlock the door to my apartment and walk inside, sighing at the comfort of my own four walls. I chuck the file down on the coffee table in my living room. Coffee is what I need right now. I make myself a pot before settling down on the sofa and delving into the file. I thought the moment I got home, my mind would stop, but it's all over the place. All I can focus on is that damned kiss.

My phone rings, breaking my concentration. I dig it from my pocket and see Scarlet flash up on the front. I swipe my finger across the screen and pick up the call.

"Hey, Scarlet."

"Hey, stranger. What are you up to?" she asks.

I sigh. "I'm working on a case from home."

She laughs. "Do you ever stop working?"

I lace my fingers through my hair and gaze at the ceiling.

No.

Unfortunately, I don't know how to switch off. The exact reason why Alec, my other ex-boyfriend, broke up with me. We only dated for a short while when I returned from law school to Wynton, but it didn't last long. When I say nothing in response, she continues, "I'm in a serious need of a girl's night out. What do you say?"

I continue staring at the ceiling for a couple of moments.

A girl's night out.

Perhaps that's what I need right now. A night to let my hair down and forget about Wes. A night to break free and get drunk.

Scarlet clears her throat. "Ivy, are you still there?"

"Yes, let's do it. What time and where?"

She *squeals* down the phone. "I didn't think I'd ever get you to agree that easy." She rustles around on the other end. "Let's say at eight o'clock at Alibi? Also, Piper will be coming too."

I smile. "Yeah, sounds good. I can't wait."

She giggles. "Me neither. See you later." The line goes dead.

I sigh and press a hand to my forehead. Eight o'clock is a few hours away. What am I supposed to do with myself in the meantime? I'm going out of my mind. Hopefully, I'll be able to pick up a *hot* guy tonight to blow off some sexual frustration.

* * *

The *bass* is pumping as I head into Alibi a few minutes late. Scarlet and Piper are lingering by the bar. Scarlet is the first to notice me and waves me over.

She pulls me into a hug. "It feels like it's been *forever.*"

I laugh. "We saw each other last week."

She pulls back and grins. "Yeah, but that was only for coffee." She shakes her head. "Do you even remember the last time you agreed to a girl's night out?"

I rack my brain, trying to remember. It's been a long time since I agreed to go out. Work keeps me so busy I barely have time to do anything. "No."

Piper steps forward and gives me a hug. "This one has been going on about the fact you agreed to come out tonight." She rolls her eyes. "I'm glad you're here now, so she can stop talking about it."

I feel so guilty. I've been such a shit friendly. Instead of taking the time to enjoy myself with my friends, all I do is work.

Scarlet links her arm with mine. "We are going to make the most of tonight." She leads us toward the VIP booths right to a table with Piper's name on it.

Her family is *filthy* rich. They are billionaires who own some multi-billion-dollar public company that her brother runs. They even own their own island some-where in the Caribbean. She works at the company, too, with the rest of her family.

I take a seat next to Scarlet. The booth is already well-stocked with two bottles of champagne on ice in the center. A waiter comes over to pour us each a glass.

Scarlet raises her glass. "To a great night out."

I raise my glass and clink it against my friends before taking a long gulp of the bubbly liquid. Slowly, I can feel the tension easing from my shoulders.

"How did your father's party go the other night?" Scarlet asks.

The moment she mentions the party, I tense up. "Don't even get me started," I mumble.

"That bad, huh?" Piper asks.

I nod and take another long swig of champagne.

Scarlet scrunches her nose. "Don't tell me a seventy-year-old groped you again."

I let out a deep sigh. "The biggest asshole I've ever met mistook me for a prostitute."

Piper gapes at me. "Are you fucking joking?"

"Nope, the new partner at the firm." A warm teasing heat floods through me thinking about him and not because I'm pissed this time. "He groped me, so I slapped him."

"Holy crap. Those parties are such a pervert fest." Scarlet says.

I nod. "He didn't even apologize."

"Was it a creepy old man?" Piper asks.

"No, he's in his late-thirties and hot." This isn't what I wanted to talk about on the girl's night out. How the hell did we get on to this subject? "He's one of those guys who knows how good looking he is and is cocky as hell."

"Well, it's been a while since you've had some." Scarlet winks. "Maybe you should have a *fling* with him."

The image of him kissing me flashes into my mind. Every inch of my body tingles with the desire to feel his hands on me again. "No way," I say a little too quickly, shaking my head. My body has a much different reaction to the suggestion. "He infuriates me." Not to mention, he pushed me up against the door of his office earlier today and *kissed* me. I don't tell them that. It's too damn embarrassing that I let it happen.

"You need to let your hair down and have fun," Scarlet says.

Piper nods. "Haven't you heard that hate sex can be the best?"

I chew on my bottom lip. I'd never heard that, but I could believe it the way my body reacted to him earlier. "Can we drop it?"

Scarlet raises an eyebrow. "Okay."

"How are you and Jamie?" I ask.

Scarlet exchanges a glance with Piper. "Not great, our sex life is more or less non-existent at the moment." She takes a long sip of her champagne. "Not to mention, I keep coming home to find him jerking off to porn."

My eyes widen. "Are you serious?"

She nods. "Yeah, it's upsetting."

Piper shakes her head. "You need to ditch that asshole and find a man who takes care of *you*." She clicks her tongue. "He doesn't make any effort."

Scarlet's eyes glisten with tears.

"It's probably a blip, Scarlet. Relationships have their ups and downs, and I'm sure you two will reignite the passion." I squeeze her hand.

She smiles. "Yeah, you're right. I'm certain we'll get back to where we were before."

Scarlet and Jamie have been dating since high-school. They were the most smitten couple ever at the time. They have been drifting apart. Scarlet doesn't deserve to be treated the way he is treating her—Piper is right. Hopefully, they can sort it out soon.

"I need a holiday," Piper says. "Either of you want to jet off to my island next week?"

I laugh. "Piper, unfortunately, we're not all billion-aires, and we do have to work," I say.

Scarlet nods. "Yeah, although I wish I could." She sighs. "Maybe we can arrange something ahead of time, and I'll get the time off work. All *three* of us could." She glances at me.

"I can ask my dad, but you know what he's like," I say.

Her shoulders dip. "Yeah, when did you last have a *proper* holiday?"

I cast my mind back over the past two years. It's been a long time. "I can't remember."

"Your dad is such a hardass." Piper huffs. "What's the point of having a rich father if you can never enjoy life?"

I shrug. "He wants to teach me to work hard for what I want in life."

Scarlet interjects, "Yeah, but you don't want to be a lawyer."

I sigh as heaviness weighs on me. "No, but I don't have a choice."

"Bullshit. You always have a choice," Piper says.

Scarlet shakes her head. "Anyway, let's forget about the *shitty* parts of our life and get *drunk*." She raises her glass of champagne in the air *again*. "To friends."

Almost the moment we've finished drinking that glass, two attractive guys approach our table. The blonde one speaks, "Hey, ladies, do you mind if we join?"

Piper shakes her head. "Of course not. Have a seat."

He sits down next to Piper, and the dark-haired one

slides in next to me. This is what I wanted when I came out — a way to blow off some pent-up frustration. I turn to him and smile.

"Hey, what's your name?" he asks.

"Ivy, what's yours?"

"Dustin, are you single?"

I nod my head and take a sip of my champagne. This guy is handsome and seems nice — the perfect guy to hook up with and get Wes out of my system. The problem is, Wes is *all* I can think about. I don't even have to kiss this guy to know that it won't compare to the way it felt when Wes kissed me.

What the hell has he done to me?

Dustin keeps chatting with me, trying to flirt, but I'm not feeling it. After a short while, he gets the hint and tries it on with Scarlet. She's already told him she's got a boyfriend. It's such a *douchebag* move. Piper is getting on like a house on fire with Chad, his friend.

Scarlet leans over to me. "Are you ready to call it a night?"

"Hell, yeah." I nod. "It's late, and I've got to get to work early."

"Me too." Scarlet turns to Piper. "Piper, we've got to get going."

Piper leans away from Chad for a moment. "No problem, I'll catch you girls later."

Scarlet links her arm with mine as we walk out of the club. There are a few cabs waiting outside, so we pick one to share. She doesn't live too far from me. All the way home, she whines about Jamie. I hate to say it, but I think Piper is right. From the sounds of it, their relationship isn't healthy.

We arrive at Scarlet's place first. She pays her half of the fare and then hugs me. I watch her stumble up the stairs into her apartment. All I can hope is one of them ends it before it becomes even more toxic.

The driver pulls up in front of my apartment, and I pay my share before getting out. As I get out onto the sidewalk, it hits me how drunk I am. I stumble up the steps to my apartment, fumbling in my bag to find my keys. Then I struggle to get them in the lock. Finally, I get it open and make a beeline straight for my sofa, flopping onto it.

For some stupid reason, I check my emails, reading through a few messages from clients that piss me off in my drunken state, so I delete them. The mouse lingers over an email from Wes. The moment I see his name, my body tingles, and my panties soak through. My heart speeds up.

The sweet memories of his hard, muscular body pressing up against me, pinning me to the wall, make my thighs clench. I find my hand snaking down my stomach and into my lacy panties, thinking about him and thinking about that huge, *thick* length pressing against my lower abdomen. I *moan* loud as my fingers slide through my drenched pussy lips, before circling my aching clit.

I may hate his guts, but I *want* him. I want him more than any man I've ever wanted. The ache between my thighs won't stop until I feel every *inch* of him filling me.

I hit the reply button on his email about the case. Before I can stop myself, I'm writing up a fantasy of exactly what I want him to do to me. What he would have done to me if I hadn't run out of his office earlier?

After writing some of it up, I read through it. I allow my fingers to drift lower again and drag through my soaking wet lips, dipping my finger inside and imagining it was his finger. My whole body is wound as tight as a spring as I move my fingers in and out, wishing I'd grabbed my dildo before starting. I rub myself into a frenzied mess of desire, imagining Wes's huge cock sinking inside of me. That's all it takes. I scream his name as I come undone.

The laptop falls to the floor, but I'm too drunk and exhausted to care. I fall asleep with the power cable wrapped around my legs.

7

WES

"Good morning, Mr. Peterson. You're here early."

I nod. "Good morning, Ellen. Yes, I needed to get a head start today on the Delaney case."

She clears her throat. "Would you like me to get you anything?" Her eyebrow raises.

"No, I'll let you know if I need you," I smirk. My secretary has been hitting on me every day since I started. In normal circumstances, I would have asked her for a drink by now. Hell, I probably would have *fucked* her by now. Instead, all I can think about is Ivy Heisman. Ellen is my usual type, but she doesn't excite me at all—not like Ivy.

I sit down at my desk and start up my computer. I need to get the IT department to load my emails onto my phone because I can't check them outside of work. I pull up my emails and my heart pounds when I see Ivy's name at the top of my Inbox. It's ridiculous how seeing her name gets me all worked up. It's a response to my email about setting up a meeting to discuss the case.

Dear asshole,

It was inappropriate and unprofessional of you to kiss me in your office, but If I hadn't left, this is what would have happened.

Wes tightened his grip on my hips, holding me closer and grinding his huge cock into me hard. I moaned as he worked my skirt down my hips, leaving me standing in my panties. He spun me around and pressed his throbbing length against my ass, making my pussy wetter than it had ever been.

I ached for him. I was desperate to feel every thick inch of him stretching me. "Naughty girls get punished," he growled into my ear, before his hand connected with my bare ass.

I gasped as the thrilling pain tingled across my ass cheeks. His arms tightened around me, and he lifted me into him, carrying me to his desk and forcing me down onto my back. He worked my panties down my thighs slowly. The air teased at my bare, slick pussy.

I glanced up at him. The hungry, ravenous look in his eyes made me quiver. His fingers went to the belt on his pants, working himself free. I gasped as his thick cock sprung from his pants, hard and glistening with thick, sticky precum. The ache between my thighs increased as he moved closer to me, slowly rubbing the swollen head of him through my slick lips, bumping it over my clit and making me jolt with pleasure. He coated himself in my juices. His precum dripped onto my pussy, making a mess.

He bent over, trailing a line with his tongue right down the inside of my thigh. I whimper as he stops short of my aching pussy.

"Please, Wes," I moaned.

"That's it, baby, beg me."

I quivered at the sound of his voice. My heart rate accelerated as he teased my lips open with the tip of his tongue. His tongue swirled over my clit, making me arch toward him. I moaned deeply, enjoying the feel of his mouth against me.

Holy shit. I have to take a break a moment from reading to free myself from my pants. I'm throbbing against the zipper as I read Ivy's dirty as sin fantasy. Fuck, this girl has a way with words, forcing me to unzip my pants and free myself, not even bothering to get up and lock the door.

He worked his tongue over my clit and added a finger into my tight pussy, making me moan and buck against him. I ground against his finger, needing more from him.

"Please, Wes," I moaned.

"What do you want? Tell me, and I'll give it to you," he growled.

"I want you to fuck me."

He grabbed my hips, digging his nails into my skin, and flipped me over. I was bent over his desk, ready for him. My whole body trembled with need. "Naughty girl," he growled. "You want this huge cock stretching that pretty little cunt?"

I could barely speak past the desperate need for him. I nodded my head and felt his thick, swollen crown nudging against my entrance.

Then it ends.

Shit.

I blink a few times. The email ends there, and I'm left fisting my length and wanting more. Where the hell is the rest of the story? I growl to myself, picturing her bent over the desk for me. Her tight ass would have been high in the air and her pretty pussy nestled between her thighs, dripping and begging to be fucked.

I feel my cock pulse in my hand at the image. I move harder and faster, thinking about how good it would feel to slide every inch deep inside that tight, wet pussy. How mind-blowing it would be to feel her come all over my throbbing cock. I stroke myself from root to tip, *groaning* as the image of her wrapped around my shaft makes me swell.

My balls tingle as they fill with cum. They are heavy between my legs. It is a wonder I have any cum left after all the jerking off I've done since I kissed Ivy yesterday. What the hell possessed her to write this?

Was she drunk? I don't even give a shit. All I can think about is her words. She *wants* me. The story is proof.

My swollen length pulses in the palm of my hand, swelling more. The pressure is becoming almost *too* much to bear as I read through her words again. The thought of tasting that sweet pussy makes my balls clench. From the small taste I got yesterday, she tastes more delicious than honey.

The release is hard and fast as thick jets of white cum shoots from the tip, splattering over my desk and the file I'd been working on. I can't even bring myself to care. I'm still stroking my dick long after I've finished coming. Ivy's words run through my mind on repeat.

A noise outside the door has me softening. I force myself back into my pants and wipe the mess from my desk. I shut down Ivy's email quickly. If I reread it, I'll be hard in seconds.

I can't quite believe it. Ivy wants me as much as I want her. My growing desperation for this woman has just gotten worse—*way* worse. There's no way I'm staying away now. She's mine to *claim*. I can only imagine she was drunk when she wrote and sent this. It's the only explanation.

Ivy's secretary had been chatting with my secretary the other day when they shared coffee runs. She loves vanilla lattes, and from that crazy email, she's bound to be hungover this morning. Coffee is what she needs. I press the intercom on my phone. "Elaine, can you get me my usual coffee and a vanilla latte, please?"

"Of course, right away, *sir.*"

I glance at the clock. It is half-past eight. After the night she has probably had, I'm not expecting her to even arrive on time. She arrives a few minutes before nine. This girl has me so interested in her. I've been noticing a lot of things I wouldn't usually notice. Like what coffee she drinks, the way she laughs, and when she turns up to work. Ivy Heisman has got under my skin so *deep* I don't think I'll ever get her out.

My heart skips a beat as my email *dings* and Ivy's name appears. Deep down, I'm hoping it's the rest of that *amazing* story. I click into it, and my stomach sinks.

Dear Wes,

Please disregard the previous email. I believe there was a spam attack on my home computer.

Regards, Ivy.

I chuckle to myself.

Does she believe I wouldn't read the email or that I'd believe it was someone else writing it? It was too specific.

I'm kind of disappointed it wasn't the rest of the story. I guess we have to start where her story finished. My cock thickens at the thought of plowing into her.

She's *all* I want. My obsession that I'll *never* be able to shake.

Little does she know I've already read her sexy as sin email and jerked off picturing her fantasy. This is her secret, dirty fantasy, and I'm going to make it her reality if it's the last thing I do. There is no way she's getting out of this that easily.

8

IVY

Oh, my God.

I blink a few times, trying to clear the image from my head. My laptop had fallen on the floor. In the process, I'd accidentally sent the dirty story I half wrote to *him*. The story I didn't finish because I got so lost in getting myself off, thinking about him.

As I read through it, I can barely remember writing it. As I re-read the story, it feels like the walls are closing in around me. The gravity of what I've done hasn't sunk in yet. My deep, dirty fantasy is in Wes's damn Inbox, and there's nothing I can do about it.

My heart pounds out of my chest as I hit reply to his last email about the case. My hands are shaking as I type out a message. It's pathetic, but all I can come up with is that my home computer has been hit with a spam attack. I implore him to ignore my last email.

It's desperate, but I don't know what else to do. I click onto my deleted folder in my emails and find a few important client emails in there. Note to self, lock laptop away next time I go out drinking. How much did I drink last night?

I groan, holding a hand to my aching head. To say I feel like shit is an understatement. Wes is the reason I went out last night trying to blow off some steam. He is the reason I drank way more than I normally would, trying to forget what he did to me yesterday. Ever since we met at that party, he has had me hot and bothered. I hate him, but I want him. It's fucked up.

I glance at the clock on my living room wall. It's gone eight-thirty. I've got all of about twenty minutes until I should be at the office. There's no doubt I'm going to be late. I jump to my feet and head for the shower as quickly as I can — my head throbs as I get ready in damn record time.

I check myself in the mirror in my hallway before leaving my apartment. Luckily, I don't look as bad as I feel. Champagne was a bad idea. I swear, the bubbles make it more *lethal* than wine. My car is on the far side of the parking lot. I unlock it, dive in, and then pull out into the traffic toward the office.

The entire way there, *all* I can think about is that email. What the hell was I thinking of writing it in an email? My hands are shaking. I know the chances of him not reading my first email are about as high as pigs flying. It's *zero*. Wes doesn't strike me as the kind of guy who takes instructions well. I step into the elevator of the building, trembling still.

A crazy notion flashes into my mind. If I could get to Wes's office before him, then I could delete the email. Then I remember I'm late. He will be sitting in his office reading it right now. I groan to myself as the elevator comes to a stop.

I step out onto my floor and head as fast as I can toward my office. All I can do is hope I don't run into him today. The last person I want to see is him. My door to the office is ajar. My brow furrows as I open it.

I *squeal* at the sight of Wes leaning on my desk, holding a latte in his hands.

What the fuck?

The smirk on his face sends heat through me. It makes my insides boil, and my pussy wet all at the same time. Right now, fight or flight is kicking in. My legs are twitching to spin me around and carry me far away and out of my office.

"Morning, Ivy," he purrs. The sound of his voice

ignites a fiery *pulsing* need for him, making my thighs clench together.

If I run now, then he wins.

Calm the fuck down and act as if everything is fine.

If I let him know how much he is getting to me, then he wins.

"Good morning, Wes," I say as evenly as I can. I step past him, plastering on my best lawyer's face, and settle in behind my desk. I busy myself, getting out my things from my handbag, and ignoring him. I'm not sure what I'm hoping for. Perhaps that he'd disappear. Once finished, I glanced up at him. "How can I help you?"

The smirk on his face widens. "Hmm, I think it's how can I help *you*?" He raises an eyebrow.

"I-I don't—"

"Here." He passes me the latte.

I stare at it for a few beats until the need for coffee out rules my need to not accept anything from this man —other than a good fucking.

Shit.

My thoughts are out of control. My body tingles with need. I focus on the latte to break the tension, taking a sip.

A vanilla latte.

How the hell did he know what I drink? Maybe

Sam gave it to him to give it to me. "Thanks," I mumble.

I return my attention to him, and when I do, the grin is gone. He's got that fierce, possessive spark in his eyes that sends a shiver right down my spine. My panties are soaking wet already. At this point, I'm not even sure why I bothered putting any on. A few moments of silence tick by, and he has no intention of breaking it. I rap my fingers on my desk. "What do you want?"

There's no way he isn't here to take the piss out of me for that drunken sex fantasy email. Why else would he be here? He smiles a panty-melting smile before stuffing his hands in his pockets and drawing my attention to the *thick*, long bulge. My mouth goes dry. "Isn't it what do you want, *baby girl?*" he growls.

Shit.

My whole body heats. I want Wes. I want him more when he growls at me like that. He's like a man possessed. I squirm in my chair and *swallow* as I return my attention to his gorgeous face.

He licks his bottom lip, drawing my eyes to them. "We'll pick this up later." He turns and walks away.

I stare after him, gob smacked. We'll pick what up later? A wave of anger, frustration, and perhaps disappointment crashes into me.

What had I expected? That he would have read the story and fucked me right here over my desk. I shake my head, trying to gain some semblance of control over my hormonal urges. I'm so angry at myself for wanting him as much as I do.

His head pops back in, and my heart hammers out of my chest. I sit upright in my chair, staring at him. "Oh, and Ivy, one more thing." His eyes sparkle. "If you could send me the rest of that story before noon, I'd be grateful. I hate cliffhangers." He winks before shutting the door.

I *groan* in utter embarrassment. Thank God I hadn't finished the story. What I'd written had been bad enough. If I didn't know any better, I'd say my face was about to explode. It is so hot. I cross my arms on my desk and drop my head onto them. All that email has done has inflated his already *too* large ego.

Now he knows I want him. I get a feeling that he won't let this go, and if he keeps pursuing me, then I know I don't have the willpower to resist. My feelings for this man are more mixed up than a milkshake. I hate him. I want him. I kind of like him.

It makes no sense at all.

The click of my door opening forces me to look up. My heart skips a beat at the thought of him returning. I shouldn't get this excited about him.

It's not him. My stomach dips.

Sam is standing in the doorway, holding my vanilla latte. "Morning, Ivy, I've got your coffee."

I glance between the latte in her hand and the one Wes gave me. I'd assumed he got it from Sam. How did he know what latte I drink? She gives me a quizzical look when I don't say anything. "Are you okay?"

I nod my head. "Sorry, yes... I had a late night."

She walks over and sets my latte down on the table, frowning slightly at the other one sitting in front of me. "A late night doing what?" She raises an eyebrow.

"Girls' night out."

She smiles. "Good, it is about time you let your hair down."

I groan. "I think I let my hair down *too* much. I've got the worst headache ever."

She laughs. "You work too hard for a girl of your age, anyway." She claps her hands together. "One second, I'll be right back." She rushes away, leaving me staring at the door.

I take a sip of my latte as she walks back through the door, holding a box of aspirin and a bottle of water. "Take two aspirin, and you'll be right as rain before you know it."

"Thanks, Sam." I open the bottle of water and take the two pills. "What would I do without you?"

Ever since my mother left, Sam has been like a rock to me. She's supported me through more things than I can count. My father isn't the caring, supportive type.

She smiles. "You're welcome." She pats my hand. "And, for the record, I think you would do just fine. Let me know if you need anything else."

I sip the water, trying to focus on my work. Yesterday, I barely got anything done. The moment with Wes in his office was too distracting. Now I can't stop thinking about the email I sent to him. I can't stop thinking about doing everything in that email and more.

How the hell am I supposed to get anything done when *all* I can think about is him?

9

WES

I've lost my mind, and I'm out of control. Ivy is everything I want. The way she looked at me earlier made me harder than nails. The raw *lust* in her fiery blue eyes made me want to lift her into my arms and *take* her right there on her desk.

The ball is in my court, and I'm ready to play. I've had enough of skirting around the tension between us. Ivy is *mine*, and I'm going to make her see that tonight. The man I was before I arrived in this city no longer exists—the playboy who will never settle down. Ivy is it for me. I knew it the moment I set eyes on her, and I knew it without a double once my lips touched hers.

As I sit behind my computer, trying to focus on the case I'm working on, all I can think of is Ivy. I've got a feeling that I won't keep this job long if I don't sort myself out. I have spent most of my first week here chasing after my boss's daughter.

I've got to plan this right, though. Ivy's waiting for my next move, and I've got to make sure it's the right one. She's a woman who is usually in control. She *hates* breaking the rules. I'm going to play by the rules for her. My stomach twists as I pull up a blank email and type her email address in.

I can't believe I'm nervous—I'm never nervous. What is it about this girl that makes my heart beat so fucking fast? It's ten to five, and Ivy always goes home at five o'clock on the dot. If I don't send her an email now, then I will miss my chance.

I type in the subject.

Subject: Story Discussion.

Miss Heisman,

I want to discuss some important matters regarding the story with you this evening. Are you free to get a drink with me after work?

Regards,

Wes Peterson.

I read through it again. This is the best way to play this—act professional, and hopefully, she will agree. Even though the subject suggests that I want to discuss that hot as fuck story she sent to me in detail. Is she going to agree to go out with me? There's only one way to find out. I hit the send button and sigh.

Ivy is the first woman who has *ever* rejected me. It was fair enough, considering I pretended to mistake her for a prostitute. Probably not my smoothest move. Okay, not my best move.

She walked into that ballroom, and it was like time slowed. It had been impossible to take my eyes off her — the most beautiful and radiant woman I'd ever seen in my entire life.

That evening, I'd been watching her the entire time. I had every intention of approaching her when she locked eyes with that *boy* across the room. A possessive sense of jealousy reared its ugly head. There was no way in hell I was letting her speak to him. Instead, I grabbed her and pretended she was a prostitute. I had no idea she was my new boss's daughter. Yeah, that made it all *ten* times more complicated.

I tap my fingers on the desk, waiting for her to reply. My heart is pounding out of my chest. What the hell has this girl done to me? When I see her name pop into my Inbox, my stomach flips. I stare for a few moments at the un-opened email. What if she has rejected me again? Finally, I open it.

Mr. Peterson,

I don't want to drink this evening, but I'd be happy to get something to eat.

Ivy.

There's nothing that's going to stop this now. I've had a taste of her sweet lips, and I've touched that *tight* little pussy. Nothing can stop me from claiming her tonight. I don't care about the company policy or that she's my boss's daughter. She's everything to me.

She doesn't want to drink, which means she's still hungover from last night. It's hard to believe. She looked as stunning as ever this morning when she walked into her office. After a big night out, no one should look that good. Ivy is the exception to *every* rule.

I hit reply.

Miss Heisman,

Sounds perfect. I'll meet you out front at 5.30 pm. I'll be in a black sedan.

Wes.

I'm like a school-boy with a crush, as I wait for her reply. My eyes fixed on my Inbox, willing her response to appear like magic. Ivy makes me feel better than I have in years. I glance down at the bulge in my pants and groan. My precum has made a sticky mess of my boxers as I rub myself through my pants. I'm going to have to work this out before I meet her. Not that it will do much good. Once I'm near her again, I'll turn to stone.

I wish we could skip the dinner and go straight for *dessert*. I'm not hungry for food. I'm hungry for Ivy.

The *ding* of my emails breaks my train of thought.

See you then, asshole.

I should hate that she's calling me an asshole. Instead, a tingle ignites in my balls.

Why the hell does her calling me an asshole turn me on so much?

10

IVY

What am I thinking?

I'm in the elevator, heading down to meet Wes for a date. I must be insane. He's a partner in my father's law firm, and the company's policy is strict about dating. Also, I hate the guy. Well, maybe hate is a strong word. He infuriates me as much as he gets my pulse racing and my pussy wet.

I glance at my wristwatch. I'm a few minutes late as it has gone past five-thirty. My heart is pounding against my rib cage. After the email last night, I'm expecting him to be an asshole about it. He is going to come on strong like he has ever since we met—it's inevitable. Buried deep down inside me, that's what I want. He takes what he wants, and it's sexy as hell. He can *take* me and do what he wants.

I head out of the building and onto the sidewalk and glance around for his car.

"Miss Heisman?" A smartly dressed chauffeur asks.

"Yes."

He opens the back door to the sedan he is standing by and nods his head.

"Thank you," I say as I slide into the back of the car.

Wes looks at me with that heated look, which gets me every time. I stiffen as his gaze ignites a pulse between my thighs. The way his eyes roam over me, it's as if he's undressing me. The silence is unbearable under his intense gaze. Something tells me he has no intention of breaking that silence as the car moves.

Finally, it gets too much. "What do you want?" I ask.

He shakes his head. "The more important question is, what do you want, Ivy?"

I shiver at the way he says my name. "No, you asked me here. Tell me what *you* want to discuss."

He runs a hand through his hair. "I want to discuss the terms."

My brow furrows. "The terms of what?"

"Terms of working together and terms of sleeping together."

My heart rate quickens. I've never said I would

sleep with Wes. His cockiness never *ceases* to amaze me. "What gives you the impression I would ever sleep with you?"

His smile only widens. "Your email told me enough," he growls, moving closer to me. "You're trembling right now, and if I were to wager all I had, I'd say your pussy is soaking wet."

I clench my thighs and shake my head. "You don't know what you're—"

His fingers reach out for my arm and wrap around my wrist. "Don't pretend," he growls. "I may well piss you off, but not half as much as I turn you on."

I clear my throat. "Why do you have to be so arrogant all the time?"

He shrugs. "Sorry, it's a force of habit. The truth is, I want to *fuck* you."

My panties soak through even more. I've made a total mess of them. I clench my thighs together and almost moan at how desperate I am for him. It is ridiculous how my body reacts to him. My mind still tries to resist him, but my body wants him. "I-I'm not going to fuck you."

The smirk fades. "Your raunchy fucking email says otherwise." He sighs. "We'll discuss everything over dinner, as I promised."

I let out a long huff and stare out of the blacked-out window of his fancy car. I can't believe he has a driver, but it shouldn't shock me. He's so vain.

My panties are so wet that I'm worried I'm leaving a damp spot on the leather seat of the car. I want Wes, but I don't want to admit it to him. The moment I got in this car, I'd expected him to objectify me. I expected his hands all over me. Instead, he's keeping his distance.

The *last* thing I want is for him to keep his distance. I can feel his eyes on me as I stare out the window, trying to distract myself from him. Luckily, I had a dress in my office—one that is far *sexier* than the dress I wore to my father's party.

He clears his throat, drawing my attention to him. "You look stunning this evening."

I cock my head to one side. "Are you sure you aren't going to mistake me for a prostitute again?"

He laughs. "Do you want to know a secret?"

I raise an eyebrow at him. "What is it?"

He shifts closer to me on the seat and lowers his voice to a raspy growl. "I knew you weren't a prostitute."

My mouth hangs open as I stare at him in disbelief for a moment.

"Don't look so shocked," he purred.

"Why the fuck did you grope me?"

He chuckled. "The moment I saw you, I knew I had to get my hands on you." He shifts even closer, his voice a husky rasp. "I had to stop you from going over to that average guy you locked eyes with."

My eyes widen. "Are you kidding me?"

He shakes his head. "No one can touch you but me," he growls.

Heat rises through my body, *prickling* across my skin. Wes is only inches away from me. Close enough to smell his strong cologne and feel the warmth radiating from his body. It sends a fiery need through me and increases my desperation to have his hands on me. Learning that he stopped me from talking to that cute guy should piss me off. I can't let it, though. It turns me on the way he talks, as though he *owns* me.

The urge to straddle him right here in the back of his car is almost overwhelming. I clear my throat. "You never apologized for causing such a scene."

He smirks at me. "No, I didn't." His large hand encases my own. "Miss Heisman, I'm ever so sorry for taking what is *mine* at your father's party." He gazes into my eyes and lowers his voice. "I'm sorry for groping your tight ass and pulling your sexy body against mine. Do you forgive me?"

His fierce and hungry eyes make me melt. I want to slap him one minute and kiss him the next.

"I forgive you." I pull my hands from his grip and move away.

The car jerks to a stop outside the most expensive restaurant in Wynton.

Shit.

"I'm not dressed for this place."

He smiles at me. "Don't worry. I thought about that." His smirk widens, and he reaches beneath his seat. "I brought you this." He holds up a bag.

I take the bag and glance inside. There is a beautiful gold dress folded inside. I glance between the dress and Wes.

"Try it on," he says.

I narrow my eyes at him. "Are you telling me to strip and change right here in front of you?"

"Yes, do it *now*." The command in his voice sends a wave of desire through me.

I swallow thickly before unbuttoning my blouse. Wes watches me, unmoving. His hand settles on the thick bulge in his pants, and it spreads more heat through me. I'm getting wetter by the second.

I shift from the seat as I remove my blouse, revealing my black lacy bra. I try to grab the bag, but Wes's fingers tighten around my wrist. "Take everything off before you put it on," he growls.

My heart rate spikes as he shifts behind me and

presses his warm body into my back. His hard-throbbing length pushes into my ass. He rests his lips against my neck, making me *moan* loudly. I arch my back into him, enjoying the warmth of his body so close. "Be a good girl and do as I say," he groans.

I bite my bottom lip and undo the zip on my dress, easing it down my legs. I'm wearing a pair of lacy black panties. Wes's fingers dig harder into my hips the moment my dress is gone, and he grinds against my bare ass. I moan again, unable to stop my reactions to him.

I'm on the edge of turning around and begging him to fuck me here—in the back of his car. Wes snakes his arm around my waist, pulling me to face him. His eyes hood with pure, feral lust.

My cheeks heat at his intense attention. His eyes rake down my entire body, lingering on my exposed breasts and then further down. He licks his lips before letting go of my waist. "You can put the dress on now, sweetheart."

I hate it and love it when he calls me that. I pull the silk dress over my head and shuffle in the confined space to ease the soft silk down my thighs. My soaking wet panties are leaving a wet patch on the leather beneath me.

I hate that I can't see how it looks on me. The fact

I've not seen my outfit in a mirror makes me ridiculously self-conscious. "I'm not sure I can go in there in this."

"Don't be ridiculous. You look stunning."

I bite my bottom lip. "You're not just saying that?"

He growls and then wraps his arms around my waist. "If you want, I'll rip it off right now and *take* you here."

I shake my head. "I told you—"

"The hard to get act is getting a little old, don't you think?"

I smile up at him and shrug. "Fine, let's have dinner."

He presses a button and speaks through to the driver, "We're ready."

"Of course, sir."

The door opens, and the driver helps me out of the car and onto the street. I smooth the silk dress down over my hips. Food is the last thing on my mind right now. All I can think about is how perfect his body felt pressed against me. Tonight is going to be a long and *torturous* evening.

11

WES

"*R*eservation for Wes Peterson," I say.

The host nods. "Right this way, sir."

My hand remains firmly planted on the small of Ivy's back as we walk to our table. He takes us to a private booth near the back. I'm gagging to sit next to her. Instead, I keep my restraint and take the seat opposite.

My chance to prove to her I'm not a creep. I want her to know that I can be a gentleman. The problem is she makes me crazy with desire. It's impossible to control myself around her because she's *mine*. I'm going to claim her tonight. There's nothing that can stand in my way.

I grit my teeth together as my possessive side rises. Ivy is staring down at the menu in silence. Her red-hair looks perfect, falling around her shoulders, complemented by the gold dress.

She glances up at me with those fiery blue eyes. The usual irritation isn't present. Instead, her eyes are filled with longing. I'm not sure when she started looking at me like that, but I like it.

The thought of wrapping that beautiful hair around my fist, claiming her lips with mine, makes me harder than nails. Ever since she slid into my car, I've been hard. My boxers are sticky with my leaking precum—it is torture. I'm not hungry for food. I'm hungry for *her*.

"Ivy, I want to cut the crap," I say.

Her eyes flick up at me. "What do you mean?"

I shake my head. "We're both grown adults. That email you sent to me was *very* graphic about what you desire." I narrow my eyes slightly. "It's clear that I desire the same thing." I lower my voice so no one can overhear me. "I want to *fuck* you tonight."

She swallows thickly and says nothing. Her cheeks turn a *pretty* shade of pink as she shifts in her seat.

"Don't tell me you don't want it."

She shakes her head. "What about work?"

I frown. "What about it?"

She inhales a deep breath. "If we're going to fuck, then we can't let it affect how we act at the office."

Hearing her say fuck has me ready to jump across the table and take her here on top of it. My cock throbs in my pants, straining so hard against the zipper it feels like it will rip through the fabric. A smile tugs at my lips when I hear her admit the truth out loud that she wants me.

Why the hell does a hole open in my stomach at the same time?

All she wants is a good fuck.

Isn't that all I want? *Normally.*

Ivy is different. I can't even imagine letting her go once I've *claimed* her. No other man will go near her. I'm going to make sure she never wants another man. The thought makes me want to turn into a caveman and club any guy that so much as looks at her.

Ivy clears her throat.

"In the office, we will remain strictly professional." I smile. "Although, that means we can't fulfill the fantasy you detailed in your email." I wink at her.

Ivy rolls her eyes before biting her bottom lip. "Perhaps we can make an exception out of hours." She blushes and glances down at her menu again.

She's so vulnerable when she's not biting my head off over the way I look at her or my cocky attitude. The waitress comes over and takes our orders. She orders a medium-rare steak, *exactly* how I like it. I order the same, and her brow raises in surprise. It looks like we have more in common than she had expected.

"We should set out some ground rules." She crosses her arms over her chest.

"In the office or bed?" I ask.

She shakes her head, a small smirk playing at her lips. "In the office."

I nod my head. "Let me have it then."

Her eyes narrow. "You can't come on to me in the office again like you did that day against your door."

I hold my hands up. "Okay, what else?"

She looks surprised at how quickly I agree. "Also, no kissing or flirting in the office unless after hours and no one is around. We can't have rumors spreading, particularly not to my father."

"Agreed." Her father is a powerful man, and I don't want to get on the wrong side of him. If he learned, I was banging his daughter. Then I would probably never work in this town again.

I should have reconsidered this entire arrangement for that reason, but I couldn't. Ivy is *all* I want. I'd do anything to have her, even if my career is at risk. My career is all I've got in life, and I'd risk it for her.

I want to tell her the truth. That she's the only woman I've ever wanted this badly, but I know it would only complicate things. She's after a hot office affair, and I'm not going to turn her down—I'll take what I can get. This woman has me wrapped around her little finger. I may be a *cocky* bastard in her eyes, but she has done something to me.

"Even when we're in public together, we have to act professionally." She glances around. "You know how *fast* rumors spread in this city."

I do know. Ivy's words only make the hole in my chest widen.

I wanted to ask to join her on the other side of the booth. She's struck that through before I could ask. I lean back in the chair and try not to let it get to me.

This is a casual affair—a business transaction. It's what I'm used to. I don't do relationships. Why do I feel so disappointed Ivy doesn't want to be seen with me? I nod my head, unable to speak past the lump in my throat.

She turns her head and smiles at me. "Is that it?"

My brow furrows. "Is what it?"

"No snide remark or sexist comment? No rules of your own?" Her blue eyes hold my gaze.

I shake my head. "Nope, I think you've covered everything when it comes to the *office*." My smirk widens. "But in the bedroom, I have a *rule* of my own."

Her cheeks turn pink, and her eyes widen. "What kind of rule?"

I lower my voice again to a husky growl. "In bed, I'm in charge. You do as I say when I finally claim that tight pussy for my own. Do you understand what I'm asking of you?"

I see her shiver at my words. She licks her lips and nods.

"Good," I growl. "I'm going to make you feel things you *never* believed possible."

Her ears have turned pink now, and she can't look me in the eye. It is even more of a turn on to see how my words can make her so vulnerable.

She clears her throat. "How about we try to enjoy dinner and talk about something else?"

She's so flustered by me. I bet her panties are so wet. I want to throw some cash down on the table and get out of there right away. I'm hungry to taste her rather than the food, but I control my primal urges. "Sure."

I take a sip of wine, and she sips her water. As the night wears on, we manage to have a conversation without her trying to bite my head off. I learn she hates being a lawyer.

"Why do you do the job, then?"

She shrugs. "It was never a question of what I was going to be when I grew up. My father had mapped out my life before I could walk."

I run a hand through my hair. "That seems pretty fucked-up. What do you want to do?"

She glances up at me with wide eyes, as if I'm the first person ever to ask her. "I don't know." She shrugs. "No one has ever asked me. It's not a question I've ever considered the answer to." She bites her lip, and I know she's holding something back.

I'd heard rumors about her dad. I knew he was a hardball, but this is ridiculous. To force his daughter into a profession she hates is plain wrong. "Well, consider it now."

She gazes into her glass of water for a moment. All of a sudden, a wide, joyful smile crosses her face. I feel my stomach flip. "I love writing."

Writing.

"You want to be an author?"

She shrugs. "I'd love to be, but it's never going to happen." She shakes her head. "There's no point talking about it. It's not like I could ever *leave* the firm." Her head dips, and the smile fades.

I clench my jaw. That's bullshit. "Okay, hypothetically, if you were to be an author, what would you write?"

Her cheeks flush again, and she gazes up at me. "I have been working on a romance novel when I get the time."

I smirk. "I'd love to read it sometime if it's anything like that story you emailed me."

She turns even redder at that. "Oh, no one has ever read it. It's not good enough."

I hate hearing her putting herself down. I hate that her father has suppressed her dreams, especially since she is only twenty-three years old. She should be able to do what the hell she wants. "Don't put yourself down like that. I bet it is great."

She gives me the most beautiful smile ever and glances down at her plate. I feel anger building in my gut that her father has controlled her so much. "Ivy, it's your life, and you can't let someone else rule it. Do what makes you happy."

She places a hand against her chest. "Is that a hint of concern I hear in your voice?" She shakes her head. "I never thought I'd hear Wes Peterson be so soppy."

"I'm not soppy. It's the truth." I run a hand through my hair. "Life is *too* short. Why waste your life doing something you hate?" I take another sip of my wine. "I got into law because I love it. The thrill of standing in court and arguing the case and the thrill of winning, which I always do." I raise an eyebrow.

She laughs a beautiful, natural laugh. "There's the cocky *bastard* I know."

I don't even care that she calls me a bastard. I relish

it. I know how much she wants me. It's surprising how comfortable I am with her. She's interesting. I rarely find women I intend to sleep with interesting, but Ivy seems to be the one exception to *all* my rules.

I have a feeling that a fiery facade is one layer of many. I wonder about what makes Ivy tick. What is she hiding behind all that angry passion? I want to get to know this girl in the bedroom and outside.

Shit.

What is happening to me?

IVY

I'm ready to explode as Wes sits close to me in the back of his car. He moves his thumb in soothing circles over my back. His thigh rests against mine, and he seems so at ease. He's probably done this *so* many times.

I'm the total opposite — a mess of nerves. I never do one-night stands or hook-ups like this. It's just not like me. Wes has said nothing since we got in his car, making me more nervous. The silence hums with anticipation. My fantasy sex story is about to become *a reality.*

My thighs clench at the thought. The car rolls to a stop, and he squeezes my hand. "We're here."

I force a smile despite the nerves twisting my gut. Wes gets out and turns to help me, offering me his hand. It's shocking how much of a gentleman he can be when he's not acting like a total asshole.

As I tried to fit him to the mold I'd had him pegged to since our first meeting, he made it impossible. He was *flirty* throughout the dinner, but other than that, he was respectful—kind, even. Our conversation after the agreement about sleeping together was pleasant.

His hand entwines with my own as he walks into his building. I glance around to make sure there's no one I know can see me. He seems to notice how tense I get and stops. "Worried about being seen holding my hand?" His eyebrow raises, and he looks almost hurt.

I shrug. "One of the rules. We need to be professional in public."

He cocks his head and nods. "Fair enough." He continues toward the elevator a few paces ahead of me. If I were to call it, he seems a little pissed off that I didn't want to hold his hand.

I ignore it and step into the elevator next to him. The doors shut, plunging us into total privacy. It's less than a second before his hands tighten around my hips, pulling me into his body. I place my hand on his hard chest as he bruises his lips to mine.

I melt into him, allowing myself to give over control to him entirely. His tongue teases over my own, and I moan into his mouth. The pulse of his *huge* cock against my lower abdomen makes me gasp. He grinds into me as our bodies writhe together in the elevator. It's hard to believe I'm kissing the asshole who hit on me at the firm's party.

I hate him. I want him. I need him.

The *ding* of the elevator startles me away from him. His arms snake around my waist, and he pulls me close as the doors open. I try to push him away, worried someone will see us.

"Don't worry. We're not in public anymore. This is my floor," Wes purrs into my ear.

The entire floor?

We're on the top floor of one of the largest and most expensive apartment blocks in Wynton. I glance over at the man standing by my side. I don't know anything about him. According to my father, Wes was a big shot lawyer in New York. I'm sure the pay was better there than in Wynton, but no lawyer has this much money.

Before I can question him, his lips bruise against mine, making me melt into his hard body. His tongue is dueling with mine as he kisses me. I *moan* into him, enjoying the feel of his muscular body pressing into me. His hands grab my ass possessively, pulling me even closer.

I feel his *pulsing* length press into my lower tummy

as he grinds into me. My arms wrap around his neck. Wes lifts me onto him, forcing my legs around his waist. He pushes me higher and higher, as his tongue teases against my own, coaxing moan after moan from my lips.

I can barely focus on what he's doing as he forces my back against the door of his apartment. He fumbles to unlock it, holding me with one arm as I kiss him desperately. Finally, the lock clicks, and he forces the door open, tumbling into his apartment with me still in his arms.

He sets me down on my feet once we're inside. A fierce possessiveness is burning in his chocolate brown eyes. My thighs quiver as I let my eyes rake down his body, halting at the thick bulge in his pants.

I glance around at my surroundings, and my mouth hangs open. It's the *largest* apartment I've ever seen. My eyes return to the man who is staring at me hungrily, wondering how he owns a place like this. "Can I take a look around?"

His eyes narrow. He looks like he's considering whether to agree or pull me against him *again*. "Sure, anything you want," he purrs.

I step into the cavernous open-plan living room, dining room, and kitchen. The place has the floor to ceiling windows looking out over the city, and a vast terrace wraps the entire front of his apartment. My eyes linger on the hallway leading off the room and deeper into the place. I walk down there, exploring. Wes remains close behind me. His footsteps echoing as I poke my head into a door ajar to the left.

I *gasp*. It's a vast library with floor to ceiling bookcases and a desk to one side.

"Go inside," he growls into my ear.

I lick my bottom lip and then step inside, walking toward the bookshelves. Wes has so many books. He doesn't cease to amaze me this evening. I read a few of the book titles and chuckle to myself when I see *Pride and Prejudice*. Wes doesn't strike me as a Jane Austen kind of guy.

"What is so amusing?"

My heart skips a beat as I didn't realize he's standing so close. "Pride and Prejudice?" I raise an eyebrow.

He shrugs. "It's a classic." His eyes have that same hunger burning in them. As if he wants to *devour* me. "Does my library meet your approval?" he asks, stepping even closer. "Am I good enough to fuck you?"

My heart rate spikes, and my body floods with that teasing heat. "The fact you even own a library, or books for that matter, puts you a cut above most men I've been with."

His jaw clenches, and his eyes flash. "How many men have you been with?"

I glare at him. Did he ask me that? As if it is a normal thing you discuss when you're about to have a fling. "That is none of your business."

He steps toward me, melting me with his eyes. "It is my business. While we're sleeping together, I *own* you. No other man can touch you." He steps even closer, warmth spreading from his body into me. "Do you understand?" he growls.

My panties get wetter, and a shiver runs down my spine.

"Answer me, Ivy."

I bite my bottom lip between my teeth and nod. I never thought I'd be so turned on by the way he wants to take charge and *dominate* me. I want him to *take* me. His fingers wrap around my throat gently, and he presses his lips to mine in a searing kiss.

I melt into it, giving over to this fiery need he's ignited inside of me. A strange desire to let him do any dirty, filthy thing he wants to me is ruling me. His tongue teases against my own, stoking that fire even hotter inside of me. The gentleness of the kiss contrasts with the roughness of his hands, grabbing my ass cheeks possessively, as if he *own*s me. It makes me crazy.

I feel his *thick*ness throbbing against my tummy as he pulls me tight to him. He moves from my lips, making me whimper as he trails kisses down my neck and across my collarbone. My pussy aches to feel him inside of me. I *moan* as he cups my breasts.

My hands snake under his designer jacket, pushing it off his broad shoulders. I'm desperate to feel his hot skin against mine. I tease my fingers over the button of his shirt, and he nips at my ear with his teeth. "No," he growls, heating me in ways I never knew possible. He grabs hold of my wrist and pushes it away from his shirt. "I'm in control."

I moan as he spins me around and presses every inch of his cock into my ass. He kisses and nibbles at my neck, grinding himself against me. "Fuck, Ivy. I can't wait to *claim* your perfect fucking pussy," he groans. "Walk forward."

I step forward on trembling legs. The pulsing between my thighs is almost impossible to bear.

"Stop," he orders.

I stop right in front of the desk in his library.

His rough hands wrap around my waist. "Turn around," he breathes into my ear.

I do as he says and meet his fierce gaze. His arms tighten around me, and he hoists me onto the desk, forcing me to lie down on it. "I know this is not the desk in your story, but it'll have to do—for now."

His large hands slide up my thighs, pushing the dress up and exposing my messy, wet, lacy panties to him. He growls lowly. His fingers tease up the inside of my thighs, slowly approaching my dripping core. "You're a naughty girl, and you need to be punished," he growls, before rubbing my clit through my panties and making me *scream* in pleasure. "Fuck Ivy." His voice is a deep baritone rasp. "Your pussy is drenched for me."

I moan, gripping to the edge of the desk as I stare at him. He pushes my dress up and pulls it over my head, exposing my lacy black bra beneath. Wes drinks me in hungrily, licking his lips. "Take off your bra," he growls.

Heat teases through me as I do as he says, unhooking my bra and dropping it to the floor. His eyes darken as my full breasts spring free to his hungry gaze, and he cups them in his hands, teasing my aching nipples between his finger and thumb. I *gasp* as they tighten and harden more, arching my back toward him.

His fingers trail down my tummy and hook into the waistband of my panties, pulling them down past my knees, exposing me to him. I squirm as the air teases against my bare, wet lips.

His hands tighten around my legs, pushing me right back against the desk and exposing me to his hungry gaze. I feel his warm breath teasing at me.

My eyes widen as his tongue darts out to lick my asshole, sending naughty, forbidden pleasure racing right through me. It's so dirty, but it feels so good. His tongue travels right from my ass, parting my slick lips and slowly dragging his tongue to my clit. I moan in ecstasy, bucking my hips to feel more.

He *growls* against my pussy. "You taste sweeter than honey, baby girl."

I *gasp* as he sucks my throbbing clit into his mouth and dips a thick finger inside my tight, wet pussy. The pleasure running through me is unlike anything I've ever felt. Wes moves his fingers in and out of me as he swirls his tongue around the sensitive nub, driving me wild. I let go, losing myself to the pleasure his tongue entices.

Outside of the bedroom, this man is an arrogant asshole who I hate, but here, in private, I want to bend to his every will. A freeing, light sensation is pulsing through my veins as I *submit* control.

I buck and writhe beneath him, needing more. His hands only hold me more firmly—totally in control.

The heat is building deep within me with every flick of his tongue and thrust of his fingers. He hits the right spot with his fingers, curling them, and I *cry* out with pleasure. "Oh my God, Wes, yes."

He licks harder and thrusts faster, taking me higher and higher right to the point of explosion. The pressure inside me is ready to go off like a bomb. I writhe beneath him, trying to get more from him. His strong arms hold me down, and he moves his tongue right from my clit, through my drenched lips and back to my asshole.

"Oh... Fuck," I cry, as he circles the ring of muscles, making the pleasure even more explosive.

His tongue delves inside of me, pushing further into that forbidden place.

I *moan* deeply. It's unlike anything I've ever felt. "Do you like that, baby?" He growls, removing his tongue and releasing my legs. "Are you a dirty girl who loves getting her ass licked?"

I nod my head, staring into his *dark* eyes. He kisses me hard, letting me taste myself on his tongue before trailing kisses back down my neck. He stops at my breasts and swirls my hard, aching nipples with his tongue. I gasp as they tighten to stiff peaks under his attention.

He keeps eye contact with me as he moves lower

and lower. His breath is teasing against the spot where I *need* to feel him again. I feel his tongue flick against my clit, making me jolt. He pulls me right back to that peak of pleasure, and I'm ready to unravel for him.

His thick fingers thrust inside of me as he grazes his teeth over my clit, dragging me right back to the edge. My body trembles and shakes as he continues to work me into a *frenzy*. His fingers curl and hit the spot inside of me that makes me tense around him.

"That's it, baby. Make that pretty little pussy come all over my tongue. Let me taste your sweet, honeyed juices and come all over my fingers. Come for me, *Ivy,*" he growls.

I scream in ecstasy as waves of unmatched plea-sure *rock* through me. My orgasm spikes through me, and I come for him harder than I've *ever* come in my life. He keeps on licking and tasting me as I come down from it.

"Stand up, baby," he groans.

He pulls me into him, gripping me hard, as if I belong to him. Our lips crash together in a hot and fierce kiss, tasting my arousal on his tongue.

I feel his lips against my neck, and he teases his tongue against the spot beneath my ear. "You like me being in control, don't you?" he growls, tightening his grip on my waist. "You love me *taking* what I want and making that pretty little pussy come all over my tongue."

I moan, unable to deny it. "You're an asshole."

He laughs. "Yeah, and you love it." He shifts me around and glares into my eyes fiercely. "You love me being an asshole and taking what is *mine*. You're mine, Ivy," he growls.

My eyes travel to the enormous bulge tenting his pants. I drop to my knees and reach out for his pants zipper.

His fingers tighten around my wrist. "What are you doing?"

I bite my bottom lip with my teeth. "My turn to taste you." I smile at him.

He growls. "Do you want to suck my hard cock like a naughty girl?"

I moan and nod, gazing up at him and tugging my bottom lip between my teeth.

"Tell me how much you want it in your mouth, baby."

Heat teases through me, making me ache for him. "I want it in my mouth so bad, Wes. Please let me suck it."

He groans, letting go of my wrist. I reach for his pants and unbutton them, pulling the zip down. My heart is beating hard against my rib cage as I pull them down, along with his boxers. I gasp as his *enormous*, thick cock springs out, slapping against his shirt clad stomach. The swollen head is glistening with precum, begging for my tongue.

I close my fingers around his thick, hot girth, stroking him from root to tip. He watches me hungrily as I drag the tip of my tongue over the crown, tasting him. He groans, sinking his fingers into my hair as I wrap my plump lips around him.

"Fuck, baby girl, just like that," he growls, tightening his grip on my hair. "Be a good girl and suck on me with your pretty little mouth."

I hum around him as I bob my lips up and down his length, swirling my tongue around the swollen crown and lapping up the thick precum leaking from the tip. He groans as I take him deeper into my mouth, making his cock swell harder. I cup his heavy balls in my hand, and he grunts.

Wes stares down at me as I lick from the tip of his perfect cock right down the *velvety* underside to his balls. His balls clench as my tongue teases them, making sweet precum leak from his head. I work my way back up and suck every drop from the tip, enjoying his sweet, masculine taste.

I wrap my fingers around the base of him. They don't even reach the entire way around. I part my lips and take him as far down my throat as I can before gagging. His grunts and groans become more animalistic as I work him in and out, keeping my eyes fixed on his.

"Your mouth feels like fucking heaven, Ivy," he groans, tightening his fingers in my hair and guiding his cock deeper.

I take more into my throat, relaxing and breathing through my nose. My pussy gushes as I take him as far as I can without gagging. The way he takes control makes me hungrier for him.

He controls the speed and force without pushing me too far. His thick head twitches against my tongue as I swirl it around his head. Hot precum spills onto my tongue, coating it with his salty taste. A sign he is close to spilling right down my throat. I want to taste him. He pulls me off, untangling his fingers from my hair, but I haven't had enough.

I pull my lips back onto him and take him right into the back of my throat. Wes roars as his balls clench, and he releases all of his cum down my throat, coating my tongue in his hot, sticky seed. I moan and swirl my tongue around his head, lapping up every drop.

His arms wrap around my waist. He lifts me into him. "I'm in control, naughty girl," he growls. "You weren't supposed to make me cum."

I pout at him, wrapping my arms around his neck. "But, I wanted to swallow every last drop, though."

He groans. "You're so dirty, Ivy." He kisses me hard, tangling his tongue with my own and tasting his essence. His hand grips my throat, making my throbbing pussy *ache* for him. "Bend over the desk, now," he orders, slapping my ass and sending a pleasurable sting through my entire body.

My eyes travel to his length to find he's still as hard as steel. My thighs quiver at the thought of him stretching me and filling me with *every* inch. I turn and walk toward the desk, bending over slowly and baring myself to him.

I did hate Wes Peterson. But right now, I love the way he commands me. I love the way he makes me feel. It's a very conflicting feeling, but I never want this to stop.

13

WES

I know I'm fucked. Ivy is off-limits, and I've crossed the line. Scratch that—I've totally and utterly obliterated the line. She's my boss's daughter, and I'm staring at her perfect, pink, glistening *cunt* nestled between her creamy thighs as she bends over my library desk.

I fist my hand up and down my hot, throbbing cock, moving closer to her. Who knew she would love being ordered around in the bedroom? Her feisty blue eyes have turned *lusty* ever since we made it into the elevator.

My hands tease over both her ass cheeks, making her gasp. "I've been thinking about slapping this perfect little ass ever since we met," I growl.

She tenses as I bring my hand back and let it land

on her ass cheek. She *moans* as a pink mark stings across her creamy skin. I massage the pink flesh of that cheek before slapping her other cheek. "Do you like getting your ass slapped?"

She nods and whimpers.

I slap her ass again, and she *cries* out with pleasure. Her pussy is dripping down her thighs. It's almost impossible to believe how wet I get her. This woman has ignited something deep and dark inside of me. I *groan* at the thought of sinking every thick inch inside those perfect, pretty lips.

I part her slippery wet entrance with my swollen head, coating her with my sticky precum. It doesn't matter that I came two minutes ago, I'm as hard as a fucking rock.

Ivy *cries* out in pleasure as I bump the thick crown over her throbbing nub before running it through her slippery lips again, teasing her.

She whimpers. "Wes, please…"

I slap her ass, making her gasp. "What do you want, baby girl?" I growl, gripping her ass cheeks with my hands possessively. "Tell me what you want."

She bucks her hips backward, trying to sink inside her sweet pussy. I grab her hips, stopping her from moving. "Tell me what you want, Ivy," I groan, fighting the urge to thrust into her deeply.

"I want you to fuck my pussy right *now*," she moans.

I bite my lip and try to fight the urge to lose it and fuck her hard and fast. "You're such a naughty girl, Ivy." I slap her ass again.

She tries to buck back into me. "I'm your naughty girl, asshole," she gasps.

I groan. "That's right. You're *mine*. This perfect little pussy is mine." I rub her clit, making her moan. Then I move my hands up her belly and grip her perfectly full breasts, squeezing them in my hands. I tease her hard nipples with my fingers, making her gasp. "These beautiful breasts are mine." She moans even louder and tries to push back into me. "This pretty little asshole is mine," I say, moving back and bending down to lick her hole.

My hands find her hips again, and I slide my leaking cock through her wet entrance, coating myself in her arousal. "Are you ready to feel every inch of me *claiming* you?"

"Yes, please, fuck me."

That's all it takes. I *growl* as I thrust right inside her tight, slick pussy. Her beautiful arousal swallows every inch of me, pulling me tight inside of her. She feels like heaven—so tight and wet. My balls ache for release, filling with cum.

Ivy moans and whimpers, trying to buck her hips and grind into me. My fingers dig into her hips, holding her still. "Remember the rules, Ivy. I'm in control." I slap her ass, and she *gasps*.

She holds still and stops trying to grind onto me. I pull slowly out of her beautiful pussy until only my throbbing head is inside her. With one quick thrust, I bury myself deep inside her again, letting her feel every inch.

I drive into her repeatedly and my blood is roaring through my veins. My heart pounds against my rib cage.

I'm used to being in control *all* the time. With Ivy, I can feel it slipping. I can feel the desperate need to claim and mark this woman driving me wild. I reach around to tease her clit as I plunge inside with one stroke, both of us *groaning* together. My heavy cum filled balls slap against her as I drive right to the hilt.

I pull out of her. "Turn around," I order.

She stands on trembling legs, turning to face me. My lips crash into hers, and I kiss her hard, tangling our tongues together. Her fingers reach for the buttons on my shirt, and I freeze beneath her. I grab her wrists, stopping her. "I'm in control."

Her eyes flash with that feisty fire, and she shakes

her head. "I'm naked." She bites her bottom lip. "I want to see you naked, *too*."

I search her eyes for a moment — a sudden vulnerability spreading through me like a disease. Women see my scars all the time, but for some reason, Ivy seeing them makes me nervous. I swallow hard, letting go of her wrist. I watch her as she continues to unbutton my shirt.

Her eyes widen as she sees the scars on my chest, pushing the shirt off to reveal every single one. Ivy traces her finger across the one on my right pectoral, making a shiver travel down my spine.

She opens her mouth, and I know she's about to ask about them. I tighten my grip on her hips and pull her to me hard, silencing her with a kiss. She *moans* into my mouth and melts into me, gripping onto my arms to steady herself.

I hoist her up, forcing her to wrap her arms around my neck. I keep my hands on her round ass cheeks and lift her perfect, dripping pussy inches from the swollen head, standing upright and ready.

Her eyes hold mine as I lower her onto my straining length, stretching her around me. I lift her up and down my length, gripping her ass cheeks tightly.

Her full breasts bounce with each thrust, and her

hard-pebbled nipples rub against my chest, making me harden more.

Her lips sear to mine, and she *moans* into my mouth. I move toward the shut door, forcing her back against the wood to help hold her. Her tongue tangles with my own, kissing me with such passion as I drive as deep inside of her as possible.

"Fuck, Wes," she moans as I fuck her harder.

Every thrust, forcing her closer. I can feel her tight walls clamping down tighter on my cock, milking the cum from my balls.

She pulls her lips from mine and glares into my eyes. The lust and pure, unadulterated desire makes me swell inside of her. My cock is throbbing for release. I move to the rug in the center of the room and sink to my knees with her, remaining buried inside her. I place her back on the floor and move above her.

She cries out as I pull right out, teasing her clit with my swollen head and then sinking right back in again, so my balls slap against her ass. Ivy watches the space where we meet as I sink in and out of her. I can tell she's close as she whimpers and moans beneath me.

"That's it, baby, take my big, thick cock right inside that hungry little pussy," I groan, slamming into her even harder and making her back arch.

"Oh God, yes," she moans, tightening her grip on my shoulders.

My thrusts become harder and more frantic as I *pound* into her. My balls slap against her ass as I pull all the way out to drive right back in, making her *scream* in pleasure. Her mouth falls open, and her eyes roll back in her head. "Oh, my God…"

I thrust in hard, bumping my swollen head against her clit with each plunge. Her already tight pussy tightens. "That's it, baby, make that naughty little cunt come all over my hard cock. I want to feel you squeeze me as you come. I want to feel your cum dripping down my balls," I growl.

Her lips part on a loud moan as she comes undone. I thrust inside her harder again, and she *cries* out.

"Come for me, Ivy. Come while I pump you full of my seed," I growl.

"Oh my god," she screams as she comes undone — her body convulsing as her orgasm tears through her. Her sweet juices drip down my shaft and right onto my balls, teasing them to release.

"That's it, baby, tease all the cum from my balls. I'm going to fill you up with so much cum it will be dripping out of you for days."

I roar as she tightens harder around me. My balls clench as they release my thick cum deep inside of her.

I keep thrusting in and out, forcing out every drop and marking her as *mine*.

Ivy is panting, and her face is flushed a beautiful shade of pink as she gazes up at me.

I shift onto my back, slipping my glistening, wet length from her messy pussy. My eyes watch as my thick white cum spills from her lips. I wrap my arms tight around her waist and pull her into me, forcing her to rest her head against my chest. Both of us are breathless and silent. My heart pounds in my ears as I hold her close.

After minutes of silence pass, she glances up at me. "That was fucking amazing."

My lips curl into a satisfied smile. "Of course it was." I wink. "What did you expect?"

She shakes her head and giggles sweetly. "Don't be such a cocky asshole."

I shift and kiss her lips. "I'm afraid you're going to have to get over it and accept that is how I am," I tease.

I tighten my arms around her waist and shift her into my lap, sitting up to kiss her neck. She *moans* as her legs wrap around my waist. Her pussy settles against my dick, which is swelling already. It feels so natural holding her in my arms. I don't know what this girl has done to me. Sex is normally fucking awkward afterward, but with Ivy, everything is different.

Ivy wraps her arms around my neck and gazes into my eyes. This woman has ignited something inside of me. Something I never believed I'd feel. It scares the fuck out of me.

She looks more beautiful than ever as she flicks her tongue over her swollen lips. Her cheeks are the perfect shade of pink, and her fiery red hair is messy. Ivy moves closer, kissing me tenderly. I allow my tongue to tangle with hers, intensifying the kiss.

Before I know it, she's grinding her slippery, wet pussy all over my swollen cock. My balls ache for more.

She raises her hips, allowing my dick to spring upright. My heart skips a beat as she slides her wet heat right over the swollen head, wanting more. I groan against her soft skin as she rises and falls slowly. I've got a feeling we won't get much sleep tonight.

14

IVY

I wake the next morning to the light pouring through the floor to ceiling window of Wes' bedroom. I roll over and settle my hand on his side of the bed. It is *cold*. His masculine scent still lingers on the sheets. I find myself drawing in a deep breath, savoring his scent.

The memories of the night before come racing back. I've never had such a hot, passion-filled night with anyone. We fucked *three* more times after the first, before falling asleep in a tangled mess in his bed. It was the best sex I've ever had. The only problem is, I'm exhausted.

It was foolish not to use protection, but I'm on the pill, so I know accidental pregnancy isn't a worry. I've never bypassed it with someone I'm not in a committed relationship with before, though. The heat of the moment caught me out. I can't help but feel a twinge of disappointment that Wes isn't here for a repeat this morning.

My eyes scan the room and I notice a garment bag, a pair of high heel designer shoes, and a toiletry bag at the end of the bed. I push the duvet off me and swing my legs over, getting out to see what he has left for me.

I can't understand how he got this done before I woke up. Perhaps he has clothes and supplies stashed here ready for *all* the women he brings home. I can't understand why my stomach knots at the thought. That's what I want, isn't it? A hot office affair with an arrogant but sexy man. No strings attached.

I shake my head and grab the toiletry bag. After last night, I've got to have a shower. I don't intend to turn up at the office reeking of sex. I head for the door on the left and find a huge en-suite bathroom.

He's got a *giant* two-person bathtub and a huge waterfall shower. I step inside the shower and turn on the water, letting it cascade over me. I think about Wes as I run my hands across my body, thinking of the way his touch felt. Before I know it, my whole body is aching for him.

I can't stop thinking about how good he felt inside

me. I force myself out of the shower after a while and return to the bedroom.

The garment bag catches my attention, and I pull my lip between my teeth, wondering what is in there. I take out the garment. It's a stunning navy-blue suit with a skirt. Similar to what I'd typically wear to work, but I can tell it's expensive. The fabric feels amazing. I try it on, and it fits me, before trying on the shoes, which are also a *perfect* fit.

I glance around, wondering where Wes is. The scent of strong coffee catches my attention, and I head out of his room toward the kitchen. A small woman in her fifties stands in the kitchen.

"Good morning, I'm sorry I was looking for Wes."

She turns and smiles at me. "He already left for work. I'm Heather, his cook, and he asked me to get you anything you'd like this morning."

I stand there a moment, trying to process what she said. How the hell does he afford a cook? Wes is *filthy* rich beyond the usual partner at a law firm.

"Coffee?" she asks, holding out a steaming mug.

I step toward her and take it. "Thank you." I take a long sip and sigh. It's the best damn coffee I've ever tasted.

"Would you like me to cook you anything for breakfast?" she asks. "I can make you some pancakes."

My stomach *rumbles* in agreement. "Sure, I'd like that."

She smiles at me and turns her attention to whipping up some pancakes. I sit in comfortable silence, watching her work, and sipping my coffee.

Once ready, she sets them in front of me. "Is there anything else I can do for you?"

I glance up at the woman. "Can I ask you a question?"

She nods.

"How does Wes have all of this?" I glance around at the apartment. "I know my father's firm pays well, but not this well."

Her lips play into a slight smirk. "You don't know who Wes Peterson is?"

I shake my head. "What do you mean?"

She pats my hand. "Perhaps that's a question you should ask Wes, dear."

I sigh. I'm not sure I want to ask Wes. It's best to keep things about sex and not our personal lives. I dig into the pancakes as Heather busies herself cleaning the kitchen. They are the best pancakes I've ever had. I need to steal his cook, not that I could afford her. Maybe he would lend her to me for a while.

As I contemplate asking him, Heather turns around

and speaks, "It's nice to see Wes has a woman over. It's the first time."

My brow furrows. "Hasn't Wes only just moved here, though?"

She nods. "Yes, he brought me with him from New York."

My eyes widen as I chew the last bit of my pancakes. Heather steps forward and grabs the plate and cutlery from me. "Now, you don't want to be late for work."

I nod absentmindedly. Still bowled over by the news that Wes never has women sleepover at his place. I clear my throat. "If you don't mind me asking, how long have you worked for Wes?"

She turns and smiles. "It will be coming up to ten years at the end of July."

I almost choke on my coffee. "And, in all that time, you've never seen Wes have a woman stay over?"

She shakes her head. "*No*. You're the first."

A strange fluttering in my stomach ensues. Is this just sex for Wes? If she is right, and I'm the first woman he has ever allowed to sleepover.

The intensity of the night was beyond anything I've ever experienced. I assumed that is rooted in the forbidden aspect. The risk made it hotter, but is it possible Wes feels something for me?

I push the notion from my mind. It's a stupid one.

"Now dear, you best get going if you want to make it to work on time." Heather stares at me. "Wes informed his driver to wait for you out front and take you in."

I smile, standing. "Thank you for breakfast."

She nods. "It was nothing. Have a lovely day, dear."

"You too." I step toward the elevator and tap my foot, waiting for it to arrive.

A *ding* sounds, and I get in. My mind is reeling with so many questions. Questions about who the hell Wes is and how he has so much money. Questions about his feelings toward me. If it's true, and I'm the first woman to sleepover in the ten years since Heather has worked for him.

I should head into work, but I know there's no point. I won't get anything done. Instead, I text my dad to let him know I'm not feeling great, and I'll be working from home. He may not like it, as I've been working from home a lot this week, but I don't care. The thought of seeing Wes around the office after last night makes me hot with embarrassment.

Even though I won't be in the office, I have a feeling it's going to be impossible to focus on anything other than Wes.

15

WES

a hot, possessive heat is consuming my entire body as I wait. I'm sitting in the conference room, rapping my fingers against the table, waiting for *her.* I haven't seen Ivy since Friday morning when I left her sleeping in my bed. That was *three* days ago. I'm going out of my mind, but she didn't come into work that Friday.

I never want to see the women I sleep with again. Ivy is different. She's the exception to the rules — the first woman I've ever let sleepover at my place. There's one thing I'm sure of ever since we slept together. She's *mine.* I've claimed her, and I'm not letting another man near her. Ivy is what I want, and I *always* get what I want.

What the hell has she done to me?

The swing of the door opening pulls me from my thoughts. My head snaps up, and my stomach dips as the accountant, Roger, walks in and sits down at his seat—not Ivy.

The danger of wanting her doesn't seem to matter anymore. Sure, her father could ruin my entire career, but I don't care. She's *all* that matters. She's the one woman I'm not allowed, but she's *all* I want.

I glance at the clock. Two minutes until the meeting starts, and Ivy's not here yet. If there's one thing I've learned from watching this girl since I started here at the Heisman firm, it's that she's always early. Where the hell is she?

I grind my teeth together and tap my foot against the floor. It feels like I will lose my mind if I don't see her.

The whoosh of the door opening again draws my eyes up. The tension eases from my shoulders as my eyes land on her. She's as beautiful as ever. Her fiery red hair is falling over her shoulders in natural curves, and her eyes are twinkling in the bright light of the room.

Those eyes meet mine for a beat, but she looks away. I have to stifle a growl rising in my chest as she takes a seat as far away from me as possible. She's avoiding me. I grind my teeth together and clench my fists. It's all I can do to stop myself from grabbing her out of her seat and pushing her against the wall right here.

Arthur, a senior partner at the firm, clears his throat. "Thank you for being here on time. I want to discuss…"

That's all I hear before I zone out, keeping my eyes glued to Ivy. The hot possessiveness that had been clawing at me ever since I made her *mine* intensifies. She looks like a goddamn angel. Her cheeks are flushed, and her lips pursed against the end of the pen in her hands.

I feel my cock thicken and throb at the memory of those perfect, pouty lips wrapped around my swollen crown as she tasted me. I *groan* internally. My precum is soaking into my boxers as I keep my eyes on her.

She shifts and writes notes on her notepad as Arthur speaks. She's the only one writing notes, and it's so damn cute. I've been staring at her, and she still won't meet my gaze. I know how obvious I'm being, but I don't give a shit. Ivy's *mine,* and I want everyone to know it.

Before long, Arthur's wrapping things up, and I haven't heard a damn word he said the entire time. "Thanks to all of you for being here. We'll catch up on this again soon." He claps his hands together.

Everyone stands from their seats, except me. I watch Ivy as she packs away her notepad. Everyone else has left by the time she's slung her bag over her shoulder. The two of us are *alone* — *my* dick pulses at the thought. I stand from my seat and walk toward her. She whirls around, not looking at me, and heads for the door without a word.

I rush after her and pin her against the door before she can yank it open. "Why are you ignoring me?" I growl into her ear.

She trembles against me. "The most important rule," she gasps out, licking her bottom lip. "Be professional while at work." She ducks under my arm and yanks the door open, escaping from me. Her hips and ass sway as she walks away.

I growl and then storm after her. Every two strides she takes, I cover in one. She's heading straight for her office.

Perfect.

I follow her down the hallway. She picks up the pace, glancing over her shoulder at me. An exciting thrill runs through me as I chase her down. She may think she's in control here, but I intend to show her just how out of control I can *make* her. She can't walk away from me like that. As if this means nothing.

Isn't that what I wanted?

Fuck.

What is wrong with me?

She rounds the corner, and by the time I make it to her door, it's shut—but not locked. I smile to myself. If she wanted to keep me out, she would have locked it. I grab the doorknob and swing it open without knocking.

She *gasps* as I throw the door open, slamming it and turning the lock behind me. I slowly turn to face her. Ivy's already sat behind her desk. Her face is pink and flushed in the most delicious way, and she tugs her bottom lip between her teeth. The heat in her eyes makes the aching need for her almost painful.

I had to see her. I had to touch her. A mind-numbing need to be near her has ruled me ever since we met.

She clears her throat, tucking a loose strand of red hair behind her ear. "Mr. Peterson, how can I help you?"

I growl, a low throaty noise that makes her flinch in her seat. "You know what I want."

Her eyes widen, and she glances down at her desk, turning redder by the second. "We agreed to keep this strictly—"

Before I can reconsider what I'm doing, I've stormed over to her side of her desk. My arms wrap around her curvy waist, and I pull her into me possessively. Our lips crash together in a hard, bruising kiss. She melts in my arms, *moaning* into my mouth and locking her hands around my neck.

The echo of footsteps outside the door has her trying to move away, but I hold her tight. "I've locked the door," I whisper into her ear.

Her fiery eyes meet mine with a mix of longing and uncertainty. "We aren't supposed to—"

I silence her with a hard kiss, forcing her to moan into my mouth again. My arms tighten around her waist, and I hoist her onto the edge of her desk.

She *gasps* as my hands snake up her bare thighs, pushing her tight as fuck skirt up to her hips to reveal her soaking wet panties. "You're so fucking naughty, Miss Heisman. Your panties are so wet," I groan, rubbing my fingers through the damp cotton.

She bites her lip to stop from crying out. I kiss her neck and below her ear, making her tremble and moan. Her hands grip onto my shoulders, pushing me lightly. "Wes." Her voice is sterner. "We agreed we wouldn't do this *here* at work."

"I locked the door, baby. No one will catch us."

She opens her mouth to reply, but I kiss her again. My tongue darts against her own, teasing and tasting her. I'll never get enough of Ivy. *Never.* She melts and wraps her arms around my neck, pulling me closer.

I part her legs with my knees, pushing my body between her thighs and grinding every inch against her. She gasps my name, "Wes."

I drop to my knees in front of her, and her eyes go wide. Her thong barely covers that perfect glistening pink pussy nestled between her thighs. I *groan*, as I trace my fingers up her creamy soft skin and then hook them under the thin strip of fabric and push it aside. Her slippery wetness coating my fingers before I've touched her. Slowly, I trace the outer lips of her pussy with my finger, teasing around her throbbing, hard clit.

She *moans* loud and then clasps her hand over her mouth.

I smile at her as she stares down at me. "That's it, baby, moan for me while I make this pretty little pussy come while we're in your office."

She stifles her moans with her hand. I slide one finger deep inside of her, and she bucks against me. I lower my mouth closer to her, ready to taste her sweet juices again, allowing my breath to tease over her clit.

"Please, Wes." she begs.

I raise an eyebrow and look up at her. "What do you want, Ivy?

She groans, biting her bottom lip. "Your tongue on me," she hisses.

I chuckle and then move my lips closer, clamping them down around her clit. She bucks wildly as I circle her clit with my tongue and then drag the tip of it right down between her wet lips, tasting her. I can't get enough of how sweet she tastes. I grab hold of her thighs and push her further onto the desk so that I can see her tight little asshole. My tongue teases over the tight ring of muscles, making her *gasp*.

Slowly, I drag the tip of my tongue back through her slit and delve inside of her lips, tasting her more deeply. She squirms above me, moaning.

It feels like I've been spiraling out of control for the past three days, and finally, I'm grounded. With Ivy here, squirming above me, I feel sane.

I return my tongue to her center, circling the tip around her clit before grazing it with my teeth. Ivy *moans* loudly and then claps her hand over her mouth, making me smile. She bites her full bottom lip between her teeth, wrestling with the need to stay in control and the desire to give in and submit to me like she did at my apartment.

I dip my thick fingers right to the knuckle into her tight, wet arousal, groaning at how good she feels. She bucks against my fingers, trying to grind me deeper inside of her. I kiss and tease at her clit as I thrust my thick fingers in and out slowly at first, building the pressure inside of her as I hit that spot that makes her gasp.

"Oh my God, Wes..." she moans *louder* than she should.

My balls tingle and ache for release at the sound of my name on her lips. She's close. I can feel the muscles fluttering around my fingers as I lick her clit harder, thrusting my fingers in and out faster. "That's it, baby. Make that tight pussy come all over my fingers here in your office. I want to taste your sweet cum on my tongue," I growl.

"Fuck," she cries out into her arm, muffling the sound as her body convulses. She comes around my fingers, tightening around them.

Fuck.

I want to be buried deep inside her right now. Her sweet juices spill onto my tongue, and I lap up every drop, savoring the taste of her. I remove my fingers from her messy, wet pussy and lick the juices from them.

Ivy watches me and moans. I stand to my feet and move my lips to hers, letting her taste herself on my tongue. Her hand reaches for the bulge in my pants, and she strokes, making me groan as I leak into my boxer briefs. I bite her lip and pull away. "We'll continue this tonight. Come to my place after work," I growl.

"Wes, I'm not sure——"

I crash my lips into hers, silencing her. I bite her full, swollen bottom lip between my teeth. "Remember, Ivy. I'm in control." I grab hold of her hips possessively, pulling her off her desk and into my body. "Now, be a good little girl and meet me outside after work." I lean towards her ear and whisper, "I want to feel you take me into your pretty little mouth before I fuck you so hard you can't remember your name."

She moans, gasping as her heavy breaths fill the room. I pull away from her, leaving her watching me as I unlock her door and leave. She didn't agree, but I know she won't disappoint me, not after the way I just made her come. Tonight, I'm going to make sure she can never resist me again. Tonight, I'm going to claim her and ruin her for any other man.

I'm trying to keep my arrogant facade in place, but I can feel it slipping. The longer I pursue her, the harder it's going to be to keep my guard up around her. She makes me want to drop it. She makes me want to open up to her, which is too dangerous. I can't allow anyone in. It's my number one rule.

IVY

I'm in over my head with Wes. The way he makes me feel is like nothing I've ever experienced. At twenty-three years old, I've had my fair share of relationships and casual sex. Nothing has ever come *close* to what Wes does to my body.

It's a *bad* idea to continue sleeping with him. Especially as I don't seem to be able to control the feelings rising inside of me. My father could ruin him if he found out. He'd never work in law in this state again.

I've never been a risk-taker, but the way he made me come on my desk was the most thrilling experience I've *ever* had. He makes me feel alive and *free*.

The problem is, it's not just sex for me. I think I knew that from the start. The way he gets under my skin and pisses me off so easily is fiery and hot. It's turning to something other than hate——something *very* different.

Friday morning, when I woke in his bed to find he'd got me a change of clothes and toiletries, something shifted inside of me. It was sweet. I wonder if he feels the same way I do.

I shake my head, chuckling to myself. There is no way Wes wants me the way I want him. He's a playboy. He's renowned for fucking women and breaking their hearts. I know if I continue to fuck him, I'm going to get hurt.

I bite my bottom lip between my teeth. The problem is, now I've started, I'm *hooked*. He has sunk his claws so deeply into me I'm not sure I can shake him off.

My phone *buzzes* against my desk, breaking my thought pattern. It's a text from an unknown number, but I know who it is. My whole body heats.

I can't stop thinking about what I'm going to do to you later. Not too long now.

Me: How the hell did you get my number?

Wes: A man has to keep his secrets. It's only an hour until the end of the day. Do you want to get out of here now?

Me: No, I'm busy.

Wes: Busy thinking about my cock?

My jaw clenches at his arrogance. What would he say if I said I was busy thinking about how this isn't just sex for me? Would he run for the hills? When I don't text back, my phone buzzes again.

Wes: Are you thinking about how good it will feel in your mouth? Are you being a naughty girl and thinking about how I'm going to sink every inch inside your soaking wet pussy and make your cum drip all over my balls?

I clench my thighs together. It's ridiculous the way by body response to him, even from a text. My panties are soaking wet and my pussy *aches* for him. I moan and slide my fingers up my thighs, touching myself through my sticky, wet panties.

I'm *so* ready for him. I glance up at the clock and then shrug to myself. There's no way I will get any more work done, so I shut down my computer and then type a message to him.

Me: Fine, let's get out of here now.

Wes: Good girl, I'm in the car out front, waiting for you.

I roll my eyes. He's so cocky he already knew I'd agree, but I can't help the smile that spreads onto my lips. As I pack my bag up, someone knocks at the door. "Come in," I call.

My dad opens the door, and my whole body turns numb. "Hey, Ivy, are you leaving?" His brow furrows.

"Y-Yeah, I hope that okay." I sling my handbag over my shoulder. "I'm not feeling too good, so I'm going to take the work home."

He raises an eyebrow. "You've been working from home a lot. Is there something wrong?"

I shake my head. "No, I just find I can focus better at home when I'm feeling a little under the weather," I lie.

He doesn't look convinced. "Okay, don't forget the dinner tomorrow night."

"What dinner?"

"The dinner with the partners for Independence Day. I sent a memo to you last night."

I shake my head. "I didn't get a memo."

He sighs. "I sent you one. Anyway, be at the Maddison Brasserie at seven tomorrow night. It's an important dinner, and I expect you to be there representing the firm." He turns and leaves without waiting for my reply.

I swallow thickly, realizing Wes will be there at the dinner too. The first event out of office since I slapped him at the party. The first event since I fucked him. My stomach twists at the thought.

I walk out of my office, locking my door and then

head for the elevator. I rock back and forth on my heels as the elevator descends to the bottom floor.

My body is wound up with a desperate need for him, but I've got to say something about us. If we keep fucking, it will only end in heartbreak—my heartbreaking. I step out of the elevator and march out the front door.

Wes's car is parked out the front, and his chauffeur opens the door for me. "Good afternoon, Miss."

"Afternoon," I say, slipping inside next to Wes.

"Hey, beautiful." His large hand reaches for me, pulling me into him and kissing me hard. His tongue delves into my mouth, making me moan before I catch myself. I force myself away, pushing his hands off me.

"Wes… Stop."

His brows furrow. "What's wrong?"

I swallow hard as my heart knocks against my rib cage. "I'm not sure we should keep doing this."

His eyes narrow. He shakes his head and plasters on that irritating smirk. Before, I always saw it as him being arrogant, but as I stare at him, I realize it's a mask. A facade to protect himself. "Why not, baby?" His fingers trace my neck. "Are you getting feelings for me?"

A pain pulses through me, clutching at my heart. "Don't be an arrogant asshole." I punch his arm. I can't admit to him I have feelings for him. "If my father finds out, you'll be the one who loses your job."

He shrugs. "It's worth the risk."

My heart skips a beat like a schoolgirl with a crush, hearing him say that. His fingers return to my hips, and he claws me to him possessively. His lips tease against my neck and up beneath my ear, making me melt like putty in his hands. I'm too weak to resist him. My heart may end up broken, but right now, I don't have the power to stop.

The car moves away from the building as he kisses me all over, biting at my collarbone. My pussy is soaking wet and aching for him to be inside of me again. His hands grip my ass as if he *owns* me, pulling me off the seat closer to him. "I can't wait to fuck your pussy again and make you come all over my dick," he growls into my ear.

My panties are dripping wet. Our lips crash together, and I lose myself in Wes, letting him *take* me. I'm his. There's nothing I can do to stop this. Every fiber of my being longs for him.

By the time we make it to his apartment, we're both out of breath and panting. My lips are swollen from him kissing me, and my body is on fire. He's like a wild animal clawing at me and *claiming* me.

I pull back from him as the car stops. His eyes are

hungry and fierce, almost animalistic as he stared at me.

"Are you sure this is a good idea?" I ask.

He forces his lips to mine again, ignoring my question. The driver opens the door for us, and he gets out first, turning to help me from the car. We're in his parking lot below ground. The chauffeur bids Wes goodnight, and then we get straight into an elevator. Wes presses the button for the top floor. Before it moves, his hands are all over me again.

I moan as his fingers slide under my skirt, teasing at my dripping arousal between my thighs. "You're so fucking wet for me, Ivy," he growls against my ear. "This naughty pussy is always dripping at the thought of my cock, filling it up with cum, isn't it?"

I *whimper* in his arms, rocking against his finger as he teases my slit. There's no use trying to fight this. I *need* him.

The elevator stops, and we both rush toward his door. He opens it, and then once it slams shut, he crashes into me hard. His fingers are unbuttoning my blouse as he forces his tongue into my mouth. By the time we stumble to his bedroom, I'm naked.

He lifts me into his arms, carrying me to his bed and setting me down in the middle. Blood pulses through my veins as he nudges my knees open, parting them to slide between my legs. He sucks on my hard, aching nipples, making my back arch in pleasure. Wes kisses across my chest and down my tummy, teasing lower and then back up to my nipples, working them into hard, aching peaks with his tongue.

He kisses up my neck and then across my jaw, making me moan deeply. My fingers find the buttons on his shirt, and I unbutton them, forcing the fabric from his shoulders and revealing his beautiful body marred with scars. I can't tear my eyes from them. The way he acted the other night, I got the sense they weren't something he wanted to discuss.

I pull on his belt as he kisses me, loosening it. His throbbing bulge strains against the fabric as I slide my hand in and free him from his boxer briefs. His thick cock slaps against his rippling abs, making my pussy ache with need.

The swollen crown glistens with hot, sticky precum that drips onto my belly, making me messy with his cum.

I moan and tremble in anticipation, wrapping my fingers around his hot shaft. Wes groans as I stroke him from root to tip, teasing more precum from him. I rub his length through my aching slit, coating myself in his leaking cum. He shifts to remove his pants, and I whimper as he returns and rubs the underside of his cock against my wet pussy, coating himself in my juices and bumping his thick, swollen crown over my clit.

"Fuck me," I rasp, clawing at his shoulders to pull him inside of me.

He bites down on his lip and growls. "I was going to make you come first."

I shake my head, trying to claw him inside of me. "I need you inside of me right *now*." I gaze into his eyes. "Please, Wes…"

For a moment, I wonder if he's going to insist he's in charge like before, but he nods. My thighs quiver as he eases his muscled hips toward me, pushing the tip inside. I gasp as his thick girth stretches me around him, forcing me to accept every thick, long inch of him. He groans as he settles deep inside me. His balls rest against my ass.

"You're so fucking tight, Ivy. You're so *perfect*," he groans, kissing my lips and delving inside of my mouth as he pulls back and thrusts into me again.

I *scream* in pleasure into his mouth. He continues to fuck me slowly at first, pulling back to gaze into my eyes as he plunges in and out. He watches my face as I take every inch. The fire inside of me catches the moment he fills me, and I can feel myself rising higher and higher with each thrust. His dark eyes hold my gaze, fierce hunger burning in them as he takes me and claims me.

The speed increases as he loses control. He fucks me hard and fast, clawing at my ass possessively as he pulls me closer into him. I've never been so filled and stuffed in my life as he drives deeper than *any* man has ever gone. His weight pins me to the bed, making it impossible to move as I *take* him and submit to the pleasure building inside of me.

I writhe beneath him, savoring every thrust. He bites my lip and growls. "Fuck, Ivy, take that thick cock in your tight, hungry pussy."

I *moan* at the filthy words spilling from his mouth and buck against him as he wraps his arms around my waist and lifts me into him. He keeps his cock buried to the hilt inside of me as he swivels me around, forcing me to kneel with my back to him. He kneels behind me and thrust into me, rubbing my clit as he does.

I *cry* out in pleasure as he kisses and bites along my shoulder. "Oh, my God, fuck."

He thrust hard and fast. I'm so slick and messy the wet sounds of us meeting together fill the room. One hand works at my clit as the other cups my breast, working my nipple between his fingers. It's all too much as the pressure heightens and heightens. I cry out his name, "Wes."

"That's it, baby girl. Make that tight pussy come all over my cock. I want to feel how tight you get when I make you come," he growls, speeding up his fingers as he rolls them over my clit. I buck back against him, turning my head to capture his lips with mine.

He groans into me, thrusting harder and faster. I gasp as he pinches my nipple harder. "I want to fill that naughty little pussy with my cum. I want to pump you so full of my cum you feel it dripping out of you for days," he growls.

I shatter and explode as he thrusts one last time. He roars against my neck as I feel his cum splash deep against my womb, falling over the edge with me. His heavy balls empty every drop inside of me.

We crash together onto the bed. Wes is still buried in me as he pulls me back against him. Finally, as our breathing returns to normal, he pulls his softening dick from my throbbing pussy.

We lay together in silence, my head resting on his chest as he holds me close. I run my fingers across the scars on his chest, making him shudder beneath me. I glance up at him. "I'm sorry. Do they hurt?"

He shakes his head, and his eyes mist with a far-off look.

I worry my bottom lip between my teeth and then

clear my throat. "Do you mind if I ask how you got them?"

His Adam's apple bobs as he swallows. "My stepfather was a violent drunk." His jaw clenches.

My fingers halt on the scar on his peck, and I gaze at him. "He abused you?"

He nods, grabbing my hand in his and removing it from his scars. "I don't like to talk about it."

I squeeze his hand, moving my hand onto his taught abs. "I understand. Let's talk about something else."

His eyes flash with relief, and he smiles. The muscles beneath me relax, and the tension leaves him. Up to now, I've seen Wes as a cocky, arrogant guy who thinks he can take what he wants. His vulnerability showed through for a moment there. Perhaps it is all a shield he hides behind—a way of keeping people out. There is more to Wes than meets the eye.

The biggest problem is I want to get to know the man behind the shield. I want to know the *real* Wes Peterson.

———

I WAKE the next morning to find Wes lying next to me. It is Independence Day, which means the office is shut, and it is a day off. My heart pounds out of my chest. I slept over for the second time at Wes' place, and this time he's still here next to me.

His arm is wrapped around my waist as he sleeps peacefully. My eyes drop to his chest and rake over those scars, making a tightness constrict around my heart. He is bottling up his pain and won't talk to me about it. Why would he? I'm just a fling for him.

Not only is this man off-limits to me because of company policy, but I know he won't want me. Wes doesn't settle down for anyone. I'm not his type. All those articles I found about him linked him to fashion models and celebrities. This is hot, forbidden sex with his boss's daughter.

My throat closes up around a lump, and I try to blink back the tears in my eyes. When the hell did it come to this? I hated this guy less than two weeks ago, and now I want to date him. If I quit the firm, then we could be together for real. It's a stupid notion because Wes would never want me like that.

Also, my father would disown me. The fact is, Wes is right. I'm miserable doing a job I don't even like at the law firm. He's the first person to tell me it's *okay* to want to do something else. My father forced this life on me, and it's not fair.

My stomach twist as I watch Wes sleep. His chest is

rising and falling with even breaths. Last night felt different for me. No doubt because I'm getting too attached to this man. He even told me how he got the scars, despite not wanting to talk about it. After we had sex, we talked for hours. I swallow hard, remembering his story. His life hasn't been easy.

He was orphaned at eight years old when his abusive stepfather got rip-roaring drunk and burned their house down. He'd been sleeping over at his best friend's house. I could sense the guilt in his voice, as he told me. No doubt guilty, he survived while his mom died in that house. It made my heartache for him.

He went into foster care for two years until a wealthy older couple who couldn't have children and who owned a billion-dollar oil company adopted him. He inherited their company when they passed away. As far as I could tell, Wes had no one else—no other family, only his money. He explained that he still works as a lawyer because Wes loves it, even though he doesn't need to.

All my preconceived conceptions about Wes were wrong. I'd assumed he was just a *cocky* player who enjoyed breaking hearts. Instead, it has become clear he's been wounded in the past, closing himself off to feeling anything real.

It makes my feelings even harder to deal with. I'm

falling in *love* with the man I can't have—a man who doesn't want me. Tonight, we both have to attend the dinner with my father. I can't let this thing between us become anything more than sex. It means I have to stop. I have to resist him.

Carefully, I remove his arm from my waist and lift the duvet. I slip from the warm bed, pulling my clothes on that are scattered across his bedroom. I take one long glance at Wes. My heart is aching as I step out of his bedroom, shutting the door and heading out of his apartment.

A sense of shame floods me as I ride the elevator down to the ground floor. The shame isn't rooted in what we did last night. It's because I'm sneaking out of his apartment. I can't face up to the truth yet. I'm freaked out by my feelings for Wes. Not to mention the fact he makes me want more for myself. Life had been *easy* until he stormed into it.

17

WES

"Wes, how are you?" Roger claps a hand against my back as I walk up to the bar.

I can barely listen to him. All I'm focusing on is finding Ivy. I know her father will have forced her to attend this party. I have to see her.

She *left*. When I woke to find her gone this morning, it felt like she had punched me in the stomach. Usually, when I sleep with women, I'm glad when they sneak out. Ivy is different. She's not a one-night stand.

Last night I made *love* to Ivy because she's everything to me. The way we sat up talking all night makes this more than sex. Doesn't she know how I feel about her? I told Ivy things I've never told anyone. Not even my best friend, Logan. Am I the only one feeling this deep, powerful connection between the two of us?

A flash of panic courses through me at the thought. The thought of being rejected by her. Maybe this is *just* sex to her.

"Wes, are you okay?" Roger presses.

"Sorry, Roger, yes, I'm good, thank you." I shake my head. "I've got a lot on my mind."

"How about we grab a drink and have a good time?" he suggests.

I nod, absentmindedly. My eyes scan the room, trying to find her in the sea of gray hair. Where the hell is she? I glance at my wristwatch and realize I'm twenty minutes early. I'd been so desperate to see her that I couldn't sit around waiting any longer.

Roger orders us each a jack on the rocks and hands me one. I accept it, taking a long swig of the fiery hot liquid to still my nerves. I down the entire glass and then scan the room again.

A flash of red hair catches my attention, and my heart skips a beat. She's standing at the entrance wearing a beautiful black maxi dress with a slit right up her thigh. The dress gives a teasing view of her long creamy legs. The plunging neckline gives everyone *too* much of an eyeful of her full, perky breasts. My fist clenches by my side at the thought of any other man looking at her in that way. Her hair is in a stylish bun that shows off her long, slender neck.

I feel my balls tingle as I watch her walk into the room. She's an *angel*.

I turn back to Roger. "I'll be right back. I've got to go and speak to someone."

Roger nods, turning to speak to Arthur, who is leaning against the bar. I stride through the room, dodging people as I make my way over to her. Her eyes lock with mine and widen.

I smile at her and continue to walk toward her. My stomach dips as she glances around the room and then dashes away from me. My chest tightens.

A hand claps onto my shoulder, forcing me to turn around. Jack, Ivy's dad, is standing behind me. "Wes, how are you getting on with the new job?"

I swallow hard. "It's going great, sir. I'm loving working for the firm."

He nods. "I'm glad to hear it. How are you getting on with my daughter?"

Shit.

He doesn't need to know how well I'm getting on with his daughter. "We're getting on fine. I'm sure we will be fast friends." I can feel my heart hammering against my rib cage. He doesn't need to know that I was balls deep inside of her only last night.

He nods. "Perfect, I need lawyers like you supporting my Ivy when she takes over the firm. She is, after all, my daughter and in line to take the managing partner role when I step down."

I clear my throat, trying not to let my nerves show through. "Of course, sir. Do you intend that to be soon?"

He shrugs. "It's not set in stone. I hope to retire a year or two from now."

"Well, I won't let you down. I will support Ivy in any way I can."

"Thank you, Wes." He smiles. "I think it is time to sit down for dinner. I put you next to Ivy because you two know each other already." If he knew how well I knew his daughter, this conversation wouldn't be so civil.

I'm glad that he has put me next to her, though. It gives me a chance to find out why she snuck out of my apartment. I walk toward the main table and find my name tag, right next to Ivy's. I get to stay close to her and make sure no man lays hands on what is *mine*.

The clack of heels on the restaurant floor draws my attention to her. She has that fiery look in her eyes as she stops by my side, leaning toward me to hiss into my ear, "Did you do this?"

My brow furrows. "Do what?"

She gestures at our name tags.

I shake my head. "No, your father told me he put us together because we know each other." I drag her chair out and hold it for her. "Would you calm down?"

She glares at me before sitting down. I sit down next to her and place my hand on her thigh, making her tense. She bats my hand away from her, leaning toward me. "This is a work function. Which means you have to be professional."

I sigh. "Was it professional of you to sneak out of my apartment this morning before I woke up?" I whisper into her ear. "There were so many things I wanted to do to you."

A visible tremor runs through her. She shakes her head. "I left because this is getting—"

The *clink* of metal against glass interrupts her. She glances at the head of the table where her father is speaking.

What was she about to say? My eyes remained fixed on her. I can't look anywhere else. I'm desperate to know what is going on in that head of hers.

Jack prattles on, speaking about something or other.

The only thing that has my attention right now is the stunning woman sitting next to me. Ivy is the only junior lawyer at this dinner, and she's the only woman.

It infuriates me that so many of the partners eye her up. I *hate* it. They are all dirty, old men who want to grope young women. It makes my blood boil when I see them look at her like that.

Ivy Heisman is mine. I may not be able to show it, but she is.

As Jack wraps up his speech, everyone chats. Ivy chats to Roger, who is sitting on the other side of her. I clench my jaw as she blocks me out of the conversation. Roger isn't much older than me. I'm sure she is laughing and flirting with him to make me jealous. It's working. I grit my teeth together as I try to focus on the meal.

After a few minutes, Ivy stands and excuses herself to go to the bathroom. I give it a minute before standing and chasing after her. I head down the corridor toward the bathroom, and once I'm certain no one is around, I let myself into the ladies' bathroom.

Ivy stands over the sink, breathing heavily. She looks upset, and tears are glistening in her eyes. The sound of the door shutting draws her attention right to me. She stands straight and glares at me in the mirror. "What the fuck are you doing in the ladies' room?"

I walk toward her, closing the gap between us. "I needed to see you. I needed to speak to you."

Ivy shakes her head. "This has got to stop. It was a bad idea from the start—"

My hands wrap around her hips, pulling her into me hard. She *gasps* as every inch of my hard cock presses against her backside. I kiss her exposed neck, holding her gaze in the mirror. "I hated waking up this morning to find you weren't by my side."

She bites her bottom lip. "Why?"

The vulnerability of the answer makes me pause and freeze up behind her. I can't expose myself to hurt. If I put all my cards on the table, there's no turning back. If she rejects me... I can't even think about it. Instead of telling her the truth, I spin her around. "Because I wanted to do this."

I meld my lips to hers, *groaning* against them. Her arms wrap around my neck as she kisses me back, melting into my arms. Slowly, I trace her bare thigh with my *rough* fingers, trailing up the slit in her dress to find her drenched panties beneath. She moans into my mouth as I rub her clit through the fabric.

My arms tighten around her waist, and I force her forward, walking her into one of the stalls. I turn to lock the door behind us. My fingers release my belt and the button of my pants before she's even turned to face me.

"Wes, what are you—" Her eyes widen as she gazes down at my length, glistening with precum. She licks her lips and moans.

"Do you want me to *fuck* you right here, Ivy?" I ask, watching her as pure lust melts over her face. "Do you want me to stretch that tight little pussy over this cock and make you come at this stupid, boring as fuck work dinner?"

She nods her head, biting her bottom lip.

"Turn around," I order.

She does as I say and turns around, bending over and pulling down her panties to reveal her pretty glistening pussy, ready for a good fucking. I groan as I move toward her, sliding my fingers through her soaking wet lips. She bucks her hips backward, trying to get my finger inside her. The hungry, animalistic need to claim this woman is so strong. I need her to know she *belongs* to me.

I drag the swollen head through her lips, bumping it across her sensitive nub and making her cry with pleasure. With one quick, hard thrust, I bury myself inside of her. My aching balls slap against her clit as she arches her back and makes a half-scream, half-moan.

If anyone were outside, they would have heard her, but I don't care. All I care about is making her mine. All I care about is this woman. I thrust in and out of her hard, fast and deep, driving her right to the edge with no reserve. Jack fucking Heisman can walk in here and find my balls deep in his daughter, and I don't give a shit.

Her tightness is pulling at me, clinging onto me as I thrust in and out. She bucks her hips back against me, forcing me harder and deeper inside. "Harder, Wes," she moans.

I roar against her neck, bending over to press my lips against her soft skin. I dig my fingers tighter into her hips and stand straight, plunging harder and faster inside of her. She's moaning loud. Anyone could hear what we're doing here, but neither of us care.

I spread her ass cheeks wide and circle the tight pink back hole with my fingers, teasing her. She moans, bucking her hips for me. I'm going to claim her fully— every single one of her holes—but not here.

I lace my fingers through her red hair, pulling her toward me and forcing her to arch her back. My hand circles her throat while I kiss the back of her neck, making her gasp. "You're mine, Ivy. Never forget it," I growl.

She rolls her hips back to meet each of my thrusts.

"Now make that pussy come for me, baby girl. Come all over me as I mark you with my cum."

She cries out, shuddering as I thrust in even harder, forcing her body over the edge as she clamps around me tightly. I growl as my balls clench and release, shooting rope after rope of thick, sticky cum deep inside of her. I keep thrusting until every last drop is drained from my balls.

I take a step back, pulling out of her. Her legs are trembling as she remains bent over. I memorize the image of her with my cum leaking from her messy pussy. I shove myself back in my pants, zipping them up.

As I stare at her, something inside of me snaps. A hot panic flushes through me, twisting my gut. I've fallen in love with this woman, something I vowed I'd never do. It means she can hurt me. She can crush my heart with one word. My heart knocks against my rib cage, and I freeze up. I'm like a deer caught in headlights.

She stands on trembling legs, and I do the most shameful thing—I bolt like a coward. Before she can turn around to face me, I'm gone.

I leave Ivy standing in the bathroom with my cum dripping from her slit. It's the biggest *asshole* move ever, but I can't face it. The way I feel about Ivy scares me like nothing else has for a *long* time. I want her more than anything, and that means I can get hurt. I can't risk it. I've lost too many people in my life and felt too much pain. It would kill me if she hurt me, too.

My heart beats fast as I rush back toward the restaurant. What the hell am I doing? I need to escape.

18

IVY

a flood of tears stream down my cheeks as I clean Wes' cum from my pussy. I've never felt so *used* before. He fucked me and then left without so much as a word. Even though this was always supposed to be just sex, he treated me *worse* than a common prostitute—at least they get paid.

My chest aches as though he has stuck a dagger into my heart and twisted. It hurts like hell. I let myself out of the cubicle and stand in front of the mirror. My eyes are red and my cheeks are puffy and swollen from crying. I turn the tap and run the cold water, splashing some over my face and waiting for the swelling to calm down.

I can't walk back in there and let him know I've

been crying. He can't realize how much *power* he has over me.

A sense of shame coils through me as I walk back toward the main dining room. My stomach churns at the thought of sitting next to Wes. He's the biggest asshole ever. I shouldn't have let myself feel anything other than hate for him. I clench my fists, angry at myself for letting this happen.

Wes is chatting to Arthur, one of the partners, as I sit down next to him. He doesn't even look at me. I can barely look at him without sickness twisting at my gut. Wes broke my heart in that bathroom and he doesn't give a shit. It hurts more than I'd like to admit. This is the reason why this twisted thing between us should have ended sooner, before I got hurt.

Roger's hand settles on my arm, forcing me to look at him. "Ah, Ivy, You're back."

My brow furrows as I glance down at his hand. He's been a little *too* touchy this evening, and it's making me uncomfortable, especially as he is married. "Yes." I glance down at the steak on my plate that must have arrived while I was gone. "How is the food?"

"It's lovely." He glances down at my cleavage, and my heart sinks a little. I thought Roger was safe. Normally, he's nothing but sweet and talks about his children. Tonight, he's acting like a creep.

I grab hold of my cutlery and cut a small piece of meat, forcing it into my mouth. I can barely stomach it. Food is the last thing on my mind. I want to go home and curl up in a ball.

Roger clears his throat, bringing my attention back to him. "So, Ivy, do you have a boyfriend?" He raises an eyebrow.

What the fuck has gotten into him tonight? He's making me feel sick right now.

"I-I don't have one at the moment… No." From the corner of my eye, I feel Wes' gaze on me. His body tense beside me.

"Interesting," he muses, continuing to eat.

I can't eat. I've barely touched my steak, but I feel sick and numb. All I want to do is go home. My father is circulating, chatting with the partners one by one. My heart pounds against my rib cage as I consider a *quick* exit. I'm sure I could sneak out without him noticing.

The moment I stand, my stomach dips. My father's eyes meet mine and I know there's no way I'm slipping away now.

Fuck.

I turn and walk toward the bathroom again. It's my only option and right now it beats sitting next to Wes for a moment more. I'd rather spend my entire night in there than out here with him. When we first met, I hated him. I knew what he was then. Why the hell did I ever risk my heart with an asshole like him?

The sounds of footsteps following me toward the bathroom makes my heart pound out of my chest. If Wes is following me, then I'm screwed. I glance over my shoulder and see that it's Roger. I'm not sure whether to be relieved or freaked out. "Hey, Ivy, wait up a second. I want to speak to you."

I come to a halt and turn to face him. "What is it, Roger?"

He walks right up to me, getting *far* closer than I'm comfortable with. The strong scent of bourbon lingers on his breath. I glance into his eyes, which are glazed over. He's drunk. I take a step back, but he grasps my wrist, pulling me close to him. "I know you want me, Ivy. The way you've been looking at me tonight."

I yank my arm from his grasp. "That's bullshit, Roger, you're married. What the hell is wrong with you?" I shake my head, trying to turn away and head into the bathroom.

His hands grab me again, pulling me right back to him. Cold fear slices through me at the look in his eyes. "Come on. It's clear you haven't had any in a long time. I'm offering to give you a good night." He winks.

"R-Roger, I'm not interested." My voice trembles.

"Now, leave me *alone*." I try to pull away, but he holds fast, dragging me toward the wall and pinning me against it.

"Don't pretend you're not attracted to me," He growls, pressing me against the wall hard.

"I'm not attracted to you and never have been." I spit out, writhing in his grasp. "Not to mention, you are married with kids. Now get the fuck off *me.*"

To my horror, he ignores me and his hand snakes up my thigh. I try to bat him away, but he won't stop. I'm about to scream for help when Wes appears over his shoulder, grabbing him and tearing him from me.

His fist connects with his face, knocking Roger to the floor with one punch. I gasp as blood trickles down Roger's face from his busted-up nose.

"Keep your hands off her, Roger." He steps toward him, his fist still clenched. "She said *no.*" He is about to take another swing when I catch his hand, stopping him.

"He's drunk. I think you've done enough damage," I say.

His eyes flash with something I can't detect, and his jaw tightens.

I turn back toward the restaurant to get away, but Wes grips my hand. "Where are you going?"

I pull my hand away. "I'm leaving," I say, turning

and heading back toward the restaurant. I grab my bag and don't even bother to speak to my father, who is enthralled by a conversation with Stuart, a senior partner.

A lump forms in my throat as I storm out of the restaurant. I don't care what my father wants anymore. This is the *last* straw. I'm not staying here any longer, no matter what.

The cool night air of Wynton wraps around me and calms the rage and shock flooding through my veins. Tears prickle my eyes and spill down my cheeks as I head down the sidewalk. I took an Uber here, but I feel like walking home—at least part of the way.

The echo of fast footsteps following me forces me to speed up. I know who is following, and I don't want to face him right now. I can't. The footsteps are even quicker and before I know it, a hand settles on my shoulder, stopping me. He pulls me around and forces me to face him.

Those deep eyes filled with irritation, staring at me intensely. His jaw is clenched. I try to pull from his grasp, but he pulls me into his strong embrace, holding me close. Why does he think he has the right? He fucked me earlier and left me without a word, and now he's hugging me.

I push him away and rest my hands on my hips.

"Don't touch *me*." I glare at him the way I did when we first met, only this time it's not hate that I feel, but pure heartache.

"Ivy, please don't push me away."

I snort. "Push you away? You're the one that fucked me in the toilets and left me without a word." My voice breaks at the end and I shake my head. More tears spill from my eyes down my cheeks.

"You're the one that insisted this was sex and nothing else. What did you want me to do?"

What did I want him to do? I can't even dignify that with an answer. Sure, it was just sex, but he was downright disrespectful tonight. I shake my head and continue on my path back to my apartment. It's not even worth wasting my breath over.

"Ivy, stop and talk to *me*." I keep walking and suddenly, he's sprinting past me, standing in my way. "You can't keep walking away. What is wrong?"

"You *are*. Yes, this is just sex, but there is such a thing as manners and respect. You made me feel like a fucking prostitute earlier." My throat closes as I try to articulate how he made me feel. "I-I can't do this anymore. This was a bad idea all along, and it has to stop *now*."

Wes steps toward me and pulls me close. "Is that what you want?"

It's not what I want, but I can't tell him the truth. I can't tell him that all I want is him, especially as everything is against us. Especially after he made me feel so used. We're not supposed to be together because of company policy and my dad would end his career in a heartbeat if he found out.

I swallow. "I-I know that we can't keep this up."

He sighs. "If that's what you want, then I will respect your decision, but at least allow me one last kiss."

He doesn't wait for a reply, and his lips meet mine in a soft and tender kiss. It makes my heartache more. It's cruel of him, but he doesn't understand. I've fallen for him as quickly as I hated him. Now my heart is breaking in two.

For a moment, I lose myself in the kiss and forget the shit my heart is going through. At that moment, it's just me and Wes in the world and it's perfect.

19

WES

"What the hell is going on here?" Jack's voice breaks me away from Ivy.

He followed us out of the restaurant and caught me making out with his daughter in the street. His eyes are full of rage.

Shit.

I lasted at the firm for two weeks, and now I'm sure I'm getting fired. Not that I need the job or the money. Hell, I'll take a law job at the state law enforcement bureau as long as I stay here in Wynton, near Ivy.

When the hell did I get so sentimental?

Ivy wipes her eyes and steps forward. "Nothing, father. I got heated when Wes was comforting me and kissed him. He did nothing wrong."

Why is she defending me? Especially after how I

treated her in the bathroom. My throat closes up as I remember the moment. It was shameful to leave her like that without a kiss or words. I had no idea how much my freak out earlier *hurt* her. Now I look back on it, it was fucking cold hearted.

Jack's eyes narrow as he glances between me and his daughter. "Where are you going?"

She crosses her arms over her chest. "I'm going home after being assaulted, but you wouldn't have a clue because you're too busy running your damn law firm."

Jack shakes his head. "Assaulted? Don't be so dramatic, Ivy."

Ivy trembles and her face turns red. "I'm not being dramatic. Roger assaulted me and pushed me up against a wall. If it wasn't for Wes punching him, then god knows what he would have done."

Jack rolls his eyes, and I can feel the rage building inside of me. The one man that should care for her and listen to her isn't even taking this brilliant and beautiful woman seriously. If he keeps this up, then I'll floor him like I floored Roger. I don't give a fuck who he is.

"Assault is a rather serious allegation, and I don't see any physical injuries."

That does it. "Jack, what the fuck? She's telling the truth. Roger tried to force himself on her sexually." I shake my head. "I had to floor him to get him off her. He had drunk *too* much bourbon, and after speaking with him briefly, it seems he's dealing with a rather messy divorce at the moment."

Ivy tenses in front of me, obviously unaware of what Roger has been going through. It explains why a man who seems like a nice guy stooped so low, but it is still inexcusable.

She throws her hands in the air. "I'm done."

"You're done with what?" Jack asks.

"You and your damn law firm. I'm fed up with being forced into a career I don't even want to be in. I'm not working for the firm for another *second*." She turns and heads past me down the street.

"Don't be ridiculous. I'll see you on Monday morning when you've cooled off, Ivy," Jack shouts after her.

Jack's attention returns to me and he glares at me. He doesn't even bother to go after his daughter, who has been sexually assaulted. Instead, he turns and heads back into the restaurant without another word or thought about what his daughter is feeling right now. Finally, I'm seeing how much of a *dick* her father is.

He learned his daughter has been sexually assaulted, and he didn't bat an eyelid. I'm not sure he is the kind of man I even want to work for. I can't let Ivy go home alone. It's clear she feels the same as me, or at least, she feels something.

I'm not giving up on her. My whole life I've been running, but I will not run from this. "Ivy, let me walk you home, at least," I shout, jogging after her.

She stops still and glances back at me as I offer my arm for her to take. She glares at me for a moment. "I told you, I'm not interested in continuing this."

I nod. "That's fine, but I'm not letting you walk home alone."

"Fine, I don't want to talk, though."

I grab her hand and continue walking.

She glances down at my hand entangled with hers, but she doesn't pull away. I notice her shiver as the wind picks up through town, even though it's a warm summer's evening. She hasn't got a jacket and I can see the goosebumps prickling across her skin. I let go of her hand and shrug off my suit jacket, wrapping it around her arms. She smiles at me but doesn't say anything. My hand entwines with hers again.

I've got to tell her the truth. Somehow, I'm not sure how I'm going to get the guts to do it. The thought of putting myself in such a vulnerable position makes me feel sick. We're silent the entire way back to her apartment. There is a palpable tension between us as she stops at the steps of her building and turns to face me.

"Thanks for walking me back," Ivy tries to shrug off my jacket, but I hold it against her, placing a hand on each shoulder.

Her blue eyes gaze up at me. "Ivy, I'm sorry about the way I treated you earlier, after we had sex."

She shrugs and glances down at her feet. "Don't worry about it. It doesn't matter now, anyway."

"I'm worried about it. I don't want to hurt you, *ever.*" I swallow hard. "You did amazing telling your father you're done with his company."

She snorts. "My father won't take that seriously. He'll expect me there on Monday morning, as normal."

I shake my head. "Well, don't turn up. You owe it to yourself to be happy, Ivy. No one should dictate what you do."

"I know. You're the first person to make me see that." She smiles. "I'm grateful for that, Wes. Thank you." Tears glisten in her eyes as she stares at me. "Good night."

My hands are shaking as I stand there with the truth on the tip of my tongue.

She turns to walk up the steps, but I grab her arm and pull her back to face me. "Ivy, wait."

Her brow furrows. "What is it?"

"You set out the rules when we started sleeping

together, and I believed I could follow them. In the past, sex has always been sex, but with you…" My throat closes up as pain coats the sides. "I've never felt like this before. Ivy, I don't want this to be just sex." I shake my head. "I want you for *real*."

Her eyes fill with more tears and she bites her bottom lip. "Is this a joke?"

I shake my head. "No, it's difficult for me to get close to people and when we had sex earlier, the reality of my feelings for you made me freak out. I'm sorry."

She stares at me for a few beats. "Are you saying you want this to be real?" She points between us. "You and me, together?" There's a hint of hope in her voice.

"That's what I'm saying."

Ivy flings herself into my arms and presses her lips against mine. She eradicates all my fears at that moment. The fear of rejection and heartbreak float away as her soft, plump lips press against mine. My heart swells as I wrap my arms around her waist.

She pulls back and stares into my eyes. "I didn't think you felt the same."

"I've wanted you ever since we met. I knew there was no way I could ever let you go once I'd had a taste."

She glances at her apartment door. "Do you want to come in?"

I smile, brushing a hair from her face. "I'd like that."

She leads me up to the front door and pauses. "I'll warn you, it's not as fancy as your place, and I don't have a cook."

I chuckle. "That doesn't matter. All that matters is you."

She smiles and opens her apartment building door, which is on the ground floor, and she wasn't kidding. It's *tiny*. I'm surprised that a daughter of such a wealthy man is holed up in a place like this. She has made it rather quaint, and it's tastefully decorated, exactly what I'd expect from Ivy.

"It's small, but it's all I can afford while I try to pay off my college debts."

I frown at her. "Are you telling me your dad forced you to go to law school and didn't even cover the cost?"

She nods and bites her lip. "Yeah, he said I need to learn to stand on my own two feet. It was important to him I paid my own way through college."

I shake my head in disbelief. "That's bullshit. He wanted you to be a lawyer and didn't even pay for your tuition with the money he has."

She shrugs and takes off my jacket, placing it on a hanger. I grab Ivy by the waist and push her against the wall, pressing every thick, throbbing inch into her.

She moans, pushing against my chest. "Are you sure about us?" She leans her head to the side.

I press my lips to the soft skin of her neck, kissing her. "Yes, I'm *all* in. I want you, Ivy, not just now, but *forever. You*'re mine, remember?"

She presses her lips to mine, moaning into my mouth. My tongue tangles with hers, teasing over her mouth as I *claim* her. Ivy pulls back breathless and flushed, biting on her bottom lip. "Wes, there's something I've always wanted to try before." She flushes pink.

"What is it?"

"I've wanted to try it for a while and never found someone I trusted—"

"Ivy, stop messing about and tell me what you want," I growl, biting her lip between my teeth.

She moans, arching her back. "Will you fuck me in the ass?"

I blink twice, wondering if I heard her right. My dick swells harder in my pants as I press every long inch into her, grinding myself against her. "Fuck yes, Ivy," I growl into her ear.

She trembled in my arms.

"I've wanted to fuck that perfect tight ass ever since I set eyes on it." I pull her even tighter to me, grinding against her pussy through the fabric of her dress. "I'm going to claim all your holes, baby girl, because you are *mine*."

My fingers reach around her back, unzipping the zip on her dress and forcing it down around her hips. My cock swells at the sight of her in a lacy red thong and matching bra. I take a step back, taking in her sexy body and beautiful curves.

She steps toward me, unbuttoning my shirt. Her eyes are filled with heat as she stares into my own. I groan as her hands reach for my belt and she loosens it, unbuttoning my pants and forcing them to the floor. I kick off my shoes, stepping out of my clothes.

I grab her ass possessively, pulling her into me. I kiss her hard, stealing the breath from her lungs.

She pulls back and drops to her knees in front of me. My cock is bulging against my tight boxer briefs as she rubs her hand across my throbbing length. Thick precum leaks into my boxers as she strokes me through the fabric. She holds my gaze as she hooks her finger into the waistband, pulling them down to free me. It slaps against my abs, painfully hard and wet with cum. I watch her as she wraps her small fingers around the base.

Her tongue darts out to taste the liquid from my swollen crown, making me groan. She teases me, swirling her tongue around the base of my head, forcing more cum to leak from the tip. She laps up every drop like a naughty fucking girl. "That's it, just like that, baby girl," I growl, thrusting my hips forward as she closes her lips around me. She takes me into her hot mouth and it twitches against her tongue, spilling more of my seed into her mouth.

She hums around me, slurping at the head before diving and taking it into her throat. Her full breasts bounce up and down in her bra as she takes me in and out of her mouth. I can feel the cum tingling in my balls, begging for release. Slowly, she works more of my cock down her throat, making me groan louder. "Fuck, Ivy. Your mouth feels perfect wrapped around my cock."

She moans, the sensation vibrating through me. Fuck. I can't last much longer in her mouth. I grab hold of her wrist to stop her. "Ivy, stop… I'm going to come."

She hums around me and then takes me even deeper. I roar as my balls clench and every drop of cum shoots right down her hot throat. She moans as I fill her throat with my seed, rope after rope spilling into her mouth. She pulls back, but more splashes onto her tongue and lips.

I growl, pulling her toward me and tasting myself on her lips. "You're such a naughty girl swallowing every drop of my cum, aren't you?"

She nods. "Yes, I'm your naughty girl."

"Yeah, you are." I slap her ass. "A naughty girl like you needs to get her pussy licked until she comes all over my face," I growl.

I lift her body into me and carry her to the bedroom, placing her down in the center of the bed. I rip her little thong off, dragging it past her knees and over her ankles. My fingers tease up the inside of her thighs as I admire her slippery, wet pussy, dripping onto her bed sheets and making a mess. "This pussy is fucking wet because you can't stop thinking about my cock, can you?"

She moans, teasing her own nipples with her fingers.

"That's it baby girl, play with yourself for me," I groan, watching her as I lower my mouth to her slick arousal. I part her lips with the tip of my tongue and delve inside, tasting her. It doesn't matter how many times I've tasted her, it's never enough. I'm *hooked* on her. Ivy is like my personal drug.

Her fingers tease at her nipples one by one as I lick

her pussy, slowly rising to circle her clit gently. She moans as I flick over the sensitive nub, making her back arch from the bed. Her eyes watch me with fiery lust as I run my hand up her thigh and push *two* thick fingers deep inside of her.

We groan together as I work her tight, wet pussy with my fingers, making her muscles flutter around me. The pressure inside her building the moment I enter her. I move my fingers in and out, licking and nipping at her clit.

Once my fingers are slick and messy with her juices, I move my them down and circle her tight asshole.

I press one finger against it and it slides in. "Oh my…" She bucks and moans, letting me sink a finger right insider her ass. I lick her clit and slowly move my finger in and out, making her writhe above me.

"Do you like having my thick finger stretching out your virgin hole?" I growl.

She glances down at me, eyes hooded. "Yes," she gasps.

I suck her clit into my mouth and then graze it with my teeth. She cries out as her orgasm crashes through her, and I run my tongue through her lips, lapping up every drop of her honeyed nectar.

Her chest heaves with heavy breaths as she comes

down from the orgasm. Her cheeks flushed and red. I growl, kissing her lips and letting her taste herself.

She moans, glancing down at my thick length throbbing between my legs. "Are you going to fuck me in the ass now?"

My cock jumps and I bite my lip. I don't reply, grabbing her legs and forcing her further onto her back, exposing that tight hole to me. I tongue her tight little ass, delving inside and pushing right in, working her muscles looser with each thrust.

I move my tongue from her ass and she whimpers. I flip her over, forcing her onto her knees. "Keep that perfect ass high and spread for me, baby," I growl, slapping her creamy cheeks. She bucks against me, desperate for more. "Have you got any lube?"

She nods toward the side draw and I open it, grabbing the lube out. I notice an average sized dildo and pull it out too as a very naughty thrilling idea pulses through me. I slather her hole in it and then put some on my fingers. My dick is straining and leaking precum all over her bedsheets. Her pussy floods with more of her sweet juice as I shove one thick finger inside her hole, stretching it and filling it with lube.

She *cries* out in pleasure, bucking back against my finger. My finger sinks in right to the knuckle. "Wes, that feels so good," she moans.

I add even more lube before thrusting another finger inside her hole, stretching her.

"Do you like that, baby? Do you like my fingers stretching that tight little ass ready for my *thick* cock?" I growl.

She nods, muttering something incoherent under her breath. After a few minutes, I introduce the third finger and she moans *deeply* as I stretch her. Her hole seems to relax and stretch in a way that suggests she's played with it before, probably with the dildo. The thought makes my cock thicken and get harder, leaking more cum all over her sheets.

"Do you like that, *baby girl?*" I groan, thrusting my fingers in and out, harder and faster now. "Do you like me finger fucking your ass?"

"Yes, God, yes..." Her voice is breathless. "Please fuck my ass with your big cock." She gazes back at me with her eyes full of desire and I pull her mouth to me, letting my swollen head rest between her ass cheeks. I kiss her hard, claiming her with my tongue.

I fist myself from root to tip in my hand, pouring lube over it and getting it ready. She watches me, glancing over her shoulder. "I'll go slow, baby," I groan, rubbing the swollen crown against her puckered, stretched hole. "Tell me if you need me to stop."

She nods and continues to watch as I rub the

underside of my length against her stretched hole, teasing her. She moans deeply. "Please, Wes... Please fuck my ass."

I roar and position the swollen crown in line with her tight, pink hole. I press against her and the muscles relax around me, sinking me inside.

She *gasps*, gazing back at me and biting her bottom lip. Her face is red as she stares back, barely breathing.

"Breath, baby," I say softly. "I'll wait until you're ready."

She nods, shutting her eyes and getting used to the thick head stretching her hole. I groan as her channel squeeze around me, leaking cum into her tight virgin ass.

She takes in deep breaths, relaxing and moaning. "I'm ready," she gasps.

I sink deeper into her, letting her get used to each thick inch. I reach around, rubbing her sensitive bud with my finger. She arches her back and bucks her hips, forcing me even deeper inside. I'm not even putting any pressure and her ass is swallowing me whole. It's feels better than anything I've ever felt.

She moans, rolling her hips as she takes every inch of me. My heavy balls rest against her wet pussy and I groan. The way she takes me inside her ass is amazing.

"Do you like the way my thick cock feels, stretching that tight virgin ass?"

She nods. "Yes," she gasps.

She moves, forcing me in and out of her. I groan, tightening my grip on her hips. She loves taking me in the ass and it just makes me *love* her even more.

Love.

Is that what this is? All my life I've been so closed off, I never thought I'd love anyone. As I sink deep into her forbidden passage, claiming her. I know without a doubt I love this woman.

20

IVY

I'm lost in the dirty, thrilling pleasure running through my body. It is better than I ever imagined. Wes thrusts in and out of my ass slowly, sending naughty pleasure through every nerve ending in my body.

He's lighting me up like I've never been *lit* up before. Pure fire burns through my veins, hot and all-consuming. The way my ass stretches around his *big*, throbbing shaft makes me tremble.

He grunts above me with each thrust. His heavy balls slap against my clit, sending more pleasure racing through me. I've always wanted to try this with a man, but never trusted anyone to try it with—until Wes. I'd played with my ass before, using my dildo and getting myself off, but nothing compares to this.

The *raw* feel of his hot, pulsing length plowing into me, making my body shake and tremble for more. I keep my eyes shut, my mouth hanging open from the pleasure. It's unlike anything I've *ever* felt.

"Are you okay?" Wes asks, forcing me to open my eyes and glance back at him.

His gaze is hungry, sending more heat teasing through me. "Fuck, yes. It feels *so* good." I move my hips, forcing him in and out of me quicker. He reaches beneath me and fingers my clit, making me *cry* out in pleasure. He's so impossibly hard as he fills me, stretching me so perfectly.

The hot pressure building inside of me feels different, even more intense, as he works my clit with his fingers and fucks me. I roll my hips back, needing more. Wes stops for a moment and I whimper, trying to buck against him. He holds my hips. "I've got an idea if you want to try it," he growls.

I glance back at him to see my dildo in his hands. A naughty, *filthy* thought rolls through my mind, making me groan. "What do you want to do with that?"

His eyes flash wickedly. "Would you like to feel it stretching out your pussy as I fuck your ass?"

I shut my eyes a moment, whimpering at the thought of being that *stuffed*. I nod my head. "Yes... Oh God, please."

He *groans*, wrapping his arms around my waist and pulling right out of my ass. I whimper at the loss of the full feeling. "Lie down on your back, baby."

I do as he says, lying on my back and spreading my legs wide for him. He thrusts his glistening, hard dick right back into my ass, making me moan. He leans down, capturing my lips with his and kissing me slowly, swirling his tongue around mine.

I watch as he thrusts in and out of my ass and grabs the dildo. The head of it teases against my clit. He rubs the toy against my messy lips, coating it in my juices.

"Are you ready to be filled up and stretched by *two* cocks?" He rubs the head of the dildo against my sensitive mud, making me jolt. "Do you want to be so full you can barely move?"

I nod my head, unable to speak. He moves the tip of the dildo to my slick, wet entrance and pushes it inside. His cock is still in my ass as he lets the dildo slip into my pussy. My mind turns blank as I glance down at it.

I'm so impossibly stuffed and full, I can't move. It's unlike anything I've ever felt and better than anything I've *ever* imagined. Wes moves his cock in and out of my ass, sending unmatched pressure through me. I *cry* out, wrapping my arms around his neck and pulling my lips to his. We crash together, tongues and teeth clashing as we kiss desperately.

He fucks me harder. "Fuck Ivy. You feel so tight being stuffed in both holes like a dirty, naughty girl," he *groans* against my lips.

His fingers find my clit and I can feel myself teetering on the edge of explosion. He rubs once, and I come undone. Every muscle in my body clamping down and writhing in pure ecstasy. The most explosive and mind-blowing orgasm rocks through me, sending heat pooling through me. I can barely see as my vision blurs. I'm screaming his name again and again as he continues to fuck me right through it.

He doesn't stop fucking me when I come down. Instead, he builds me right back for another one. I'm writhing and moaning as he drives in harder and faster, fucking my tight asshole. The dildo is still deep inside of my pussy. I never want this to end—the feel of him filling me so perfectly.

"Your asshole feels so fucking good wrapped so tightly around me. I want to feel you tighten around me again, Ivy." He kisses me quickly. "I want to feel you milk the cum from my balls and make me fill your tight ass with my cum."

I moan, teetering on the edge of what feels like the

most *explosive* orgasm ever. I'm not sure I've come down from the last one as he drives into me more frantically.

"Come for me, baby." He growls. "I want to feel that tight ass clamp down around me as you come hard for me."

His thumb flicks over my clit hard and I come to *pieces*. I'm not sure if I scream or moan or what I do. All I know is my body lights on fire. Heat like nothing I've ever known crashes into me, sending me reeling. My pussy gushes around the dildo still lodged inside of me.

Wes roars against my lips, kissing me as I feel him explode. I feel every drop of cum that spills from his *thick*, pulsing shaft deep in my ass, filling me up. He stops moving inside of me and rests his forehead against mine, breathing heavily above me.

We're both silent, listening to our own heavy, rasping breaths. Finally, he slips out of my ass and then removes the dildo, making me whimper at the sudden empty sensation. He wraps his arms around my waist, lifting me into his lap and kissing me tenderly.

I've never felt so loved or protected in my entire life.

I WAKE in Wes's arms. His chest rises and falls beneath me. I can't believe how quickly I've fallen in love with the man I hated so much when we first met.

Is it even real?

He promised me last night that he wants me for real. Deep down inside, I'm anxious. Wes's reputation is renowned, and he's not even from this town. According to the newspapers, he's a womanizer. A man who fucks women and leaves them, just like he did to me in that bathroom stall.

What if this is all a game to him? A flash of panic grips me suddenly, as I know I wouldn't survive the heartache. He said he wanted me forever, but men lie.

I've known that for a long time. Maybe he just wanted to fuck me and then, when he gets bored, he will cast me aside. I let him do the most intimate thing to me last night. A dull ache reminds me of that and how *good* it felt.

If this was all a game to him, then I'm not sure I could survive the pain.

My mind returns to what I said to my father the evening before and his remark. When I said it, I meant it, but I can already feel my confidence waning. Wes makes me want to give it all up and do what I want, which is scary.

What if I'm not a good enough writer to make it?

Wes stirs beneath me and shifts, waking. He glances down at me and smiles. "Morning, beautiful."

I force a smile at him despite the worry spreading through me. "Morning," I mutter.

He forces me to glance up at him. "What's wrong?"

I shake my head and sigh. "Nothing... I'm just thinking about what I said to my father," I lie, as it's not the only thing worrying me.

He smiles. "Not chickening out, are you?"

I shake my head. "I have no intention of following through. I never did."

His smile drops. "Ivy, you have to." He cups my chin in his hands. "If you don't stand up to your father and do what you want to do, then you'll never be happy."

I sigh. "What if I'm not a good enough writer?"

He smirks at me. "If that story you sent to me on email is anything to go by, I'd say you're good enough."

I laugh and shake my head. "I wrote that when I was *drunk.*"

"Even better. You're clearly a *talented* writer." He shifts and pulls me into his arms, sitting up. "The fact is, you'll never know if you don't try." He presses a kiss against my lips. "I'll stand by you every step of the way, Ivy."

My heart swells at the way he supports me. I've never had this. A man who *cares* so desperately for my happiness. A man who wants to support me, even if it might not work out. I press my lips to his. "I *love* you, Wes,"

He freezes beneath me, his body tensing. A glazed look floods his eyes as he stares into the distance.

"Don't worry, you don't have to say——"

His lips close over mine, slow and soft. When he parts from me, he leans toward my ear. "I love you, Ivy. I *love* you so much."

My heart skips a beat and I hold him tight. With Wes by my side, I feel like I can do anything.

21

WES

I keep my hand against the small of Ivy's back. She's trembling. I know this will be tough for both of us. I squeeze her hip with my other hand, trying to reassure her.

We're standing together as the elevator rises to the top floor of the Heisman firm. Jack Heisman's floor, as he has the entire top floor to himself. I have managed to persuade Ivy to stick to her guns and do what's right for her. She can't let her father dictate her life—It's not right.

The elevator dings and she glances at me, worrying her lip between her teeth. "Don't worry, baby. Everything will be okay. I promise."

She nods and smiles, taking a deep breath. "Let's do this."

I can't help but smile as she laces her hand with mine, giving me a determined look.

Jack doesn't strike me as the kind of guy who's going to accept this with any ounce of decency. But together we're unstoppable. Nothing else matters if I've got Ivy by my side.

We step out of the elevator together. Ivy squeezes my hand once more before letting go. The secretary behind the desk frowns at us. "Can I help you?"

Ivy clears her throat, striding toward her desk. "Yes, I need to see my father. Is he in?"

The recognition dawns and she nods. "Of course, Miss Heisman. I'll let him know you're here." She grabs the phone and types in a couple of numbers. "Sir, your daughter is here to see you." There is a short pause before she places the phone down on the receiver.

"You can go on in now." She nods toward the closed door.

My heart pounds hard in my chest as I walk behind Ivy. Not only am I about to tell my boss of two weeks that I'm in love with his daughter, but Ivy's about to tell him she's quitting the firm for *good*. There's no way this will be easy.

Ivy's fingers wrap around the door handle and she

hesitates for a moment, glancing back at me. I give her a sharp nod and the best smile I can manage, given what we're about to do. I close the distance between us and whisper into her ear, "I'm right here with you, always."

She smiles back at me and then twists the handle.

"Ivy, what do you want?" Jack asks, keeping his eyes fixed on his computer.

I clear my throat, making him glance up. His brow furrows. "Wes, what are you doing here?"

"We're here to discuss something with you," I say.

Jack's eyes narrow and he glances between the two of us. "Well, I don't have all day, so spit it out."

Ivy steps forward, her jaw clenched. "I'm quitting the firm for good, Dad," she says, her voice quiet.

Jack laughs. "Don't be ridiculous, Ivy. What else would you do?"

"I'm going to be a writer. It's what I've always wanted to do, but you forced me to study law."

Jack snorts. "Writing isn't a viable profession. You're in line to take over this company and goddamn it, I'm not letting it pass out of our family."

"It's my life and I want to do something I enjoy. I hate being a lawyer. I've always hated it and I'm through with it *now*."

Jack stands from his desk, knocking his chair backward. "Like hell you are. Ivy, if you don't fall in line, so help me God, I'll disown you and strike you from my will." His fingers are clenched into fists.

I step up to Ivy's side and rest a hand on her shoulder. "Jack, Ivy has a right to decide what she wants to do with her life." My jaw clenches. "No one should be able to tell her what to do."

Jack's eyes meet mine. I can see a vein throb on the side of his neck. "This has nothing to do with you." He points a finger in my direction. "Why the fuck you even here?"

Ivy's hand entwines with mine and she pulls me close.

I swallow hard, staring into the outraged eyes of my boss. "It has everything to do with me," I say, gazing down at Ivy. "I'm in love with your daughter, sir."

His face turns red in an instant. "You both lied to me the other night when I caught you kissing?" he asks, his voice a low growl.

Ivy steps forward. "I lied to protect Wes. We want to be together and it's not breaking any rules because I no longer work here."

Jack splutters, moving around the desk and charging toward me. His fists are clenched and his whole body is tense. I can see the warning signs. He wants to beat me to a pulp.

Ivy steps in front of me and glares at him. "Don't you dare touch *him*!" she shouts.

I set my hands on her shoulders, pulling her close to me. "I hope you can come around to the fact that we are together and that Ivy isn't working here anymore." I narrow my eyes at him. "Obviously, I understand if you don't want me here, either."

Jack growls. "Damn right, I don't. Both of you get the fuck out of my *sight*."

Ivy tenses and turns to face me. Her eyes fill with tears as she gazes up at me.

I turn back to her father. "Fine, we'll leave, but I don't think you know what you're doing." I shake my head. "Your daughter is a brilliant and intelligent woman. She deserves to be happy, and she deserves to do what she wants with her *own* life."

Ivy grabs my hand and shakes her head. "Don't waste your breath, Wes." Her head hangs low, and I hate to see her like this. I hate that her father doesn't give a shit about what she wants.

I glare at Jack, who is trembling with rage, before glancing down at Ivy. I give her a small nod and squeeze her hand, allowing her to pull me away.

"Don't think I won't disown you for this, Ivy," Jack growls after us.

She tenses but keeps walking, pulling me away from her father. I hadn't expected it to go smoothly. I'd expected her dad to hit the fucking roof. We just turned everything in his world upside down. But fuck him. Ivy deserves to be happy. We deserve to be happy together.

Ivy sobs the moment we're in the elevator. I wrap my arms around her waist and pull her close. "I'm so sorry, Ivy."

"It's not your fault." She shakes her head. "I knew he would be an ass about it. I guess deep down I hoped he'd understand."

"I get that. You never know, he might come around." I shrug. "We've dropped a huge bomb on him."

Ivy nods, tightening her grip on my waist. I hold her as we ride to the bottom floor. Ivy wipes her face as the elevator comes to a stop and then glances up at me with a heated look. "You know, we never made the fantasy in my story come true." She bites her lip and then presses the button on the office floor. "Since we don't work here anymore, how about we make it a reality?"

I groan as my cock thickens in my tight boxer

briefs. "You're such a naughty girl, Ivy Heisman. I think it's about time I bend you over my desk and give you a *hard* punishment." I kiss her as the elevator moves back to our floor.

The *ding* of the elevator arriving breaks us apart and, as stealthily as we can, we head for my office. Ellen isn't at her desk, so we slip inside and lock the door.

Ivy giggles as I snatch her into my arms and lift her, forcing her legs around my waist. I carry her toward the desk and set her down on it, hiking her dress up. My fingers work her waistband down her creamy thighs, exposing her perfect, glistening pussy to my hungry gaze.

I lick my lips, ready to taste her, when she grabs my hand, forcing me to look up.

"Wes, just fuck me," she moans, eyes dilated with lust.

I arch my brow. "I want to make you come, baby girl."

She shakes her head. "I need you inside of me… I need to feel you stretching me and filling me with cum," she gasps.

I groan, rubbing a hand over my straining dick. "You're so dirty, Ivy." My fingers work my belt and button loose and I unzip my pants. I let them fall down my hips, freeing myself from my boxer briefs and stepping toward her.

She trembles in anticipation, keeping her eyes fixed on my aching length. I move toward her and rub my swollen head between her folds, coating myself in her juice. I press my hips forward, pushing into her slowly.

I grip her hips, drawing her hard against me. She moans as I slip deep inside of her. My eyes remain fixed on hers as she melts with pleasure. Her plump lips fall open and her eyes glaze over as I fill and stretch her tight pussy. I remain still at first, kissing her softly and tenderly.

"Fuck me," she moans, trying to move her hips.

I grip her tightly. "Remember, baby. I'm in control," I groan into her ear.

She moans in response, arching her back. "Please, Wes, I need you to fuck me."

I growl against the skin on her neck and pull almost all the way out of her, before slamming back inside with a quick, hard thrust. Her pussy is dripping wet as I ease myself in and out of her, watching her face melt in pleasure. I love seeing what I do to her and the way her eyes blue eyes dilate.

She's watching me too. We're both staring at each other, locked in each other's gazes as we move as one. I can't tell where I start as she begins as I drive so deep inside her. Ivy's fingers lace through my hair and she pulls me close, forcing our lips together. Our tongues tangle in a heated, passionate duel as we both fight to taste each other. She caves to me, allowing me to search her mouth thoroughly and giving up control.

I get even harder as I drive in and out of her, faster and deeper, making her moan. The desk rocks beneath us and papers flutter to the floor. Neither of us give a shit, as we don't work here anymore. None of it matters anymore. All that matters right now is *us*.

Ivy bites her lip, but it doesn't stifle the sweet moans that escape them. Her pussy is tighter around my length as the pressure inside her builds, making it even more difficult for me to hold on. Thick, hot precum leaks into her pussy with each thrust. I bite her bottom lip gently, tugging it into my mouth and then sucking on it.

She *moans*, no longer trying to control the sounds she's making. We're both lost to our desire for each other.

"Fuck, Wes. I'm going to come," she *cries* out.

I grunt, thrusting into her harder and faster. "That's it baby, come while I fuck you on my desk like a naughty little girl."

The muscles in her pussy flutter around my throbbing length as she comes undone, writhing beneath me. She cries out as her orgasm rocks through her, making her pussy so damn tight it's trying to milk every ounce of cum from me.

I roar as I explode inside of her. My balls release jet after jet of cum deep inside her, marking her as mine. Our heavy breaths fill the office as we stay like that for a while, gazing at each other.

Finally, I pull my softening dick from her, letting the thick, white cum drip from her lips onto the office floor. She looks beautiful, lying on my desk, full of my cum. "That was way *hotter* than my story," she says, smiling up at me.

I turn toward the desk and grab some tissues we'd knocked onto the floor for her to clean up. "I thought your story was hot too, but reality is way better than fiction." I wink at her, passing her the tissues.

"Thanks," she says, cleaning herself up and fixing her panties back in place.

"I hope you can feel my cum dripping out of you all day," I growl, kissing her neck.

She bites her lip. "Maybe you can fill me with more when we get back to your apartment, just to be sure."

I growl and pull her to me, kissing her hard. If we're not careful, we'll end up fucking in my office all day. "Come on, let's go home," I say, grabbing her hand and pulling her out.

I don't care that I've lost my job and most likely damaged my reputation. All I care about is Ivy. We'll figure it all out—together. With her by my side, I feel unstoppable.

"Good morning, Mrs. Peterson." Wes's arms wrap around my baby bump as he kisses my neck.

"Good morning." I glance at the clock on the kitchen wall. "Aren't you going to be late for work?" It's almost nine o'clock.

He shakes his head and kneads my shoulders. "Nope, I've got the day off."

I raise an eyebrow at him. "My dad gave you a day off?" I ask.

He smiles and shrugs. "Yeah, is that so hard to believe?"

I nod, flipping the eggs in the frying pan. "I didn't get any time off in two years."

It's been a year since Wes and I met. A total whirlwind is all I can describe it as. We were married within two months and I was pregnant after another two. My father came around to the fact I wasn't going to be a lawyer and apologized for the way he spoke to us that day in his office. I'll never forgive him for forcing me into something I didn't want, but we're working through our differences.

In fact, when he learned we were getting married, he proposed a deal. Although it won't be his own child taking over the firm, he was hellbent on keeping it in the family.

My father is priming Wes to become the managing partner of the firm. I know he hopes that our children might want to take over, but that will be up to them. There's no way I'm forcing a life they don't want on them.

How do I know we're going to have more than one child? I'm carrying twins. It was frightening when I found out, but Wes has been so supportive.

Not to mention, Wes wants more children and so do I. I published my first novel last month and it's doing well. I've also been freelance writing, and I'm bringing in enough money to keep doing it full time. We don't need the money, not with Wes's millions and his wage, but I couldn't sit around doing nothing. I've never been so happy.

"Why are you taking the day off?" I ask.

He shakes his head, laughing. "You don't know, do you?"

I frown at him. "Know what?"

"Today is the one-year anniversary of the day we first met." He grabs my hand and pulls the pan off the heat, turning the hob off. "One year since you slapped me at that party." He smiles down at me.

"I think you're forgetting that you—"

He kisses me hard, silencing me. I *moan* against his mouth, feeling his fingertips dig into my ass as he claws me closer. "Happy Anniversary, baby." He grabs a box out of his pocket and hands it to me.

My eyebrow raises. "This isn't our anniversary, though. We got married ten months ago."

He smirks. "Take the box." He forces it into my hand.

I take it and undo the ribbon wrapped around it. I open the box and stare inside.

A key.

But, I'm not sure what it is for.

"I bought us a house."

My mouth falls open and I stare at him. "You did what?"

He shrugs. "With the babies coming, I knew this place wasn't right to raise children."

I blink. "You sold the apartment?"

He shook his head. "No, I'll rent it as long as you're happy with the house."

As I run the key through my fingers, I'm not sure whether to be ecstatic, or pissed he didn't talk to me about it first. Sure, it's his money. He can do what he wants with it, but it might have been nice to go searching for a house together.

Before I can respond, he speaks, "I'm sure you're going to love it. Come on." He wraps his hand around my own and leads me to the elevator.

"Where are we going?"

He laughs. "To our new home."

I glance back over my shoulder toward the kitchen. "I haven't even had breakfast yet."

He pulls me into the elevator, wrapping his arms around me and kissing my neck. "We'll get something on the way."

I sigh as he pulls me out of the door and into the elevator. He pulls me against him, digging his fingers into my hips gently. "You look beautiful today," he whispers in my ear.

I heat, moaning softly as he presses his lips against my bare shoulder. He chuckles into my ear. "Even at eight months pregnant, you can't get enough, can you?"

I shake my head. "It doesn't seem like it."

The ding of elevator breaks us away and we head for the parking lot. His driver, Carter, is waiting by his black sedan. Wes opens the door for me and I slip inside. He eases into the seat next to me, gripping my thigh tightly. "What do you want for breakfast?"

"You," I say, kissing him.

He chuckles. "You said you were hungry."

I shrug. "I'm just nervous now. How about we wait and get an early lunch on the way back?"

"Whatever you want, baby girl." He squeezes my thigh as we travel through Wynton's busy morning traffic.

My heart is pounding against my rib cage at the thought of seeing our new home. I'm still torn whether I should be annoyed with him. "Didn't you consider I might like a say in choosing our home?"

He turns his head to the side with that silly smirk on his face, the one that used to get me so riled up. "I know you well enough to know you will love this place. Trust me."

I nod and we fall into a comfortable silence. My eyes remain fixed out the window, and I wonder what's going on when Carter takes the road out of Wynton. "Where is this house?" I gaze up at him.

His smirk widens. "Be patient and you'll find out."

He's unbelievable. I keep watching out of the window for about forty-five minutes, until Carter turns off the main road and down a small, dirty track drive. I frown at him. "Surely, this commute isn't ideal for you working every day?"

"It's worth it to live somewhere beautiful. Not to mention, it's not like I drive myself, anyway."

He had a point. Carter drives him everywhere. I watch out the window as a stunning, large, modern home comes into view. I gasp at the sight of the sea over the cliff. "Oh my God."

Wes kisses my cheek. "You like it, don't you?"

I glance up at him. "I love it and I haven't even been inside it yet."

He laughs. "I bought the place when I first moved to Wynton and have had contractors working on it ever since. I wanted to keep it a surprise. My intention was always to have it as a retreat, but I reckon it would make a great family home." The car comes to a stop. "Come on, let's go." He throws open the passenger side door and helps me out, holding my hand as we continue up the path toward the front door. It's a beautiful place. Better than anything I'd never imagined.

"There's a nice little town called Waterford only a five-minute drive from here, with shops and a few diners. Not to mention, a pizza delivery service." He winks.

There's no way I can fault him with this choice. It is beyond anything I ever could have dreamed of.

"Do you want to look inside?" He asks, holding the keys up.

I snatch them from him. "That's a stupid question."

I rush up the stairs and unlock the door, throwing it open and gasping as the first thing I see is the sea view. The windows in front of me stretch the entire length of the large house. An open plan living area leads into a dining area and kitchen.

"What do you think?"

I spin to face my husband, leaning against the wall with his hands in his pockets. He's always so self-assured and confident in his choices. But, it no longer gets me angry, it only makes me love him more. "I love it."

He smirks. "Of course you do. I picked it."

I walk toward him and punch him in the arm. "Don't be a cocky asshole."

He wraps his arms around me and pulls me close. "You love it really."

I press my lips to his, certain I've never been this happy in my life. Wes freed me from a job I hated and made me realize how important doing something I truly loved was. He makes me strive for more every single day. I can't wait to give birth to his babies and start a family with him.

THANK you for reading Filthy Lawyer, I hope you enjoyed it.

If you'd like to read more, Filthy Doctor is free for signing up to my mailing list here.

You can also check out my other series, Romano Mafia Brothers. The first book in the series is Her Mafia Daddy and it's available to read with a KU subscription or to buy for $0.99

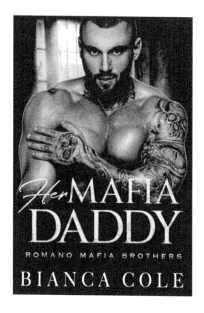

He has taken me captive, and I can't stop fantasizing about him tying me to his bed.

Kane Romano is the most handsome, powerful man I've ever met. He's also the man holding me captive.

My step-dad found himself on the wrong side of the mafia, and then offered me up in exchange for his life. How does he have the right? I'm eighteen years old, and my step-dad doesn't own me.

The problem is, Kane Romano agrees. Everyone knows you don't fight with a Romano, unless you want to end up in an unmarked grave.

I should be scared, but every time I look into those

dark eyes, I feel safe and protected. When we're alone he's a gentleman, but around anyone else he turns quiet and cold.

There's a thrill being here with him. Even though I've never been with a man, I find myself wanting him —a man who is more than twice my age and claims he owns me now.

When he asks me to call him daddy, I know I won't be able to refuse him…

ALSO BY BIANCA COLE

The Syndicate Academy

Corrupt Educator: A Dark Forbidden Mafia Academy Romance

Cruel Bully: A Dark Mafia Academy Romance

Chicago Mafia Dons

Violent Leader: A Dark Enemies to Lovers Captive Mafia Romance

Merciless Defender: A Dark Forbidden Mafia Romance

Evil Prince: A Dark Arranged Marriage Romance

Boston Mafia Dons Series

Cruel Daddy: A Dark Mafia Arranged Marriage Romance

Savage Daddy: A Dark Captive Mafia Roamnce

Ruthless Daddy: A Dark Forbidden Mafia Romance

Vicious Daddy: A Dark Brother's Best Friend Mafia Romance

Wicked Daddy: A Dark Captive Mafia Romance

New York Mafia Doms Series

Her Russian Daddy: A Dark Mafia Romance

Her Italian Daddy: A Dark Mafia Romance

Her Cartel Daddy: A Dark Mafia Romance

Romano Mafia Brother's Series

Her Mafia Daddy: A Dark Daddy Romance

Her Mafia Boss: A Dark Romance

Her Mafia King: A Dark Romance

Bratva Brotherhood Series

Bought by the Bratva: A Dark Mafia Romance

Captured by the Bratva: A Dark Mafia Romance

Claimed by the Bratva: A Dark Mafia Romance

Bound by the Bratva: A Dark Mafia Romance

Taken by the Bratva: A Dark Mafia Romance

Wynton Series

Filthy Boss: A Forbidden Office Romance

Filthy Professor: A First Time Professor And Student Romance

Filthy Lawyer: A Forbidden Hate to Love Romance

Filthy Doctor: A Fordbidden Romance

Royally Mated Series

Her Faerie King: A Faerie Royalty Paranormal Romance

Her Alpha King: A Royal Wolf Shifter Paranormal Romance

Her Dragon King: A Dragon Shifter Paranormal Romance

Her Vampire King: A Dark Vampire Romance

ABOUT THE AUTHOR

I love to write stories about over the top alpha bad boys who have heart beneath it all, fiery heroines, and happily-ever-after endings with heart and heat. My stories have twists and turns that will keep you flipping the pages and heat to set your kindle on fire.

For as long as I can remember, I've been a sucker for a good romance story. I've always loved to read. Suddenly, I realized why not combine my love of two things, books and romance?

My love of writing has grown over the past four years and I now publish on Amazon exclusively, weaving stories about dirty mafia bad boys and the women they fall head over heels in love with.

If you enjoyed this book please follow her on Amazon, Bookbub or any of the below social media platforms for alerts when more books are released.

Printed in Great Britain
by Amazon